A Cup of Coffee with My Interrogator

the Prague Chronicles of Ludvík Vaculík

Introduction by Václav Havel

translated by George Theiner

readers international

Published in English by Readers International Inc., and Readers International, London. Editorial inquiries to London office at 8 Strathray Gardens, London NW3 4NY England. US/Canadian inquiries to Subscriber Service Department, P.O. Box 959, Columbia LA 71418-0959 USA.

Free to use a Typewriter, My Philosophers, A Cup of Coffee with My Interrogator, On Heroism, Spring Is Here (1982), Thus Spake Švejk, Walking down Příkopy and *Words...* reprinted with kind permission of *INDEX ON CENSORSHIP* magazine.

Cover art and illustrations by Czech artist Jan Brychta
Typesetting by Grassroots Typeset, London N3
Printed and bound in Great Britain.

ISBN 0-930523-34-2 Hardcover
ISBN 0-930523-35-0 Paperback

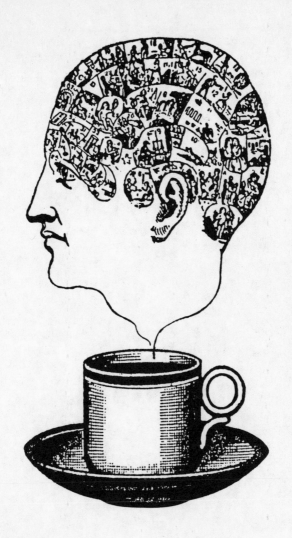

*T*he feuilleton—*a journalistic-literary genre that became very popular in Central Europe in the last few decades of the Austro-Hungarian Empire—found some very distinguished practitioners in such Czech writers as Jan Neruda and, in the 1920s and 1930s, Karel Čapek. It was revived forty years later by Ludvík Vaculík, one of the best-known Czech authors of the 1960s, who was in the forefront of efforts to humanise the communist system. His critical writings of the period culminated in the famous 2000 Words manifesto, calling for faster and more comprehensive de-Stalinisation at the height of the Prague Spring of 1968. Immensely popular with Czech readers, by the same token he became the* bête noire *of Czechoslovakia's hardliners, and so it surprised no one that he was among the several hundred writers banished from official Czech literature after the Soviet invasion.*

Unable, like so many others, to publish his work in the state-run publishing houses and official media, and unwilling to resign himself to ''writing for the drawer'', *Vaulík found a simple, yet effective solution: in the early 1970s he and some of his friends among Czechoslovakia's proscribed writers started exchanging their manuscripts, typing perhaps a dozen copies and passing them around among themselves. This led to the idea that they write regular* feuilletons, *commenting on events at home and abroad and on their own situation. Vaculík, who was the begetter of this project, has remained faithful to it to this day, still turning out at least one* feuilleton *a month.*

Over the years, these works—collections of feuilletons, *novels, plays, volumes of poetry or essays, etc.—have added up to a formidable "publisher's list" of well over 200 titles under the name of* Edice Petlice *(Padlock Publications). The books soon came to be copied by other hands and circulated among readers eager to get hold of the latest works of these forbidden authors. Other writers, such as Václav Havel and Jan Vladislav, started their own "editions", and a flourishing "samizdat industry" was born.*

In January 1977, Vaculík stood at the cradle of the Charter 77 human and civil rights movement, being arrested together with Havel and the actor Pavel Landovský, on their way in Landovský's car to post the first copies of the Charter to the Czechoslovak authorities. Though detained and interrogated innumerable times, Vaculík has been more fortunate than, say, Havel in that he has never had to spend time in prison. But, as he emphasises in his feuilleton *"A Day in August", he has never failed to speak up for what he believes to be right, has never compromised with the petty, dictatorial authorities: "If I am unable, or not allowed, to function, I have to grin and bear it. Let them get on with it. But I don't have to keep silent, that I don't!"*

George Theiner, Editor,
Index on Censorship

Contents

Introduction

by Václav Havel

The first half of the 1970s here in Czechoslovakia lives in my memory as a period of darkness. The gradual process of growing self-awareness and liberation of our society in the preceding decade and the great social upsurge of 1968 was followed by long years of frustration, depression, resignation and apathy as a consequence of the Soviet intervention and so-called "normalisation". Not that life had come to a standstill—naturally, much that is important kept on happening; nevertheless our society as a whole was atomised, the various small sources of independent activity scarcely knew of each other's existence, lacking the information and the channels of communication, the parallel structures that exist today.

All this applied in equal measure to our literature: Czech writers were soon divided into those who adapted to the new conditions, recanted their earlier views, or simply managed to get by because they had not "sinned" in the past; and those who were banned, cast out, spat upon by official propaganda. These writers turned to writing "for the drawer", eked out a living as best they could, existing in a kind of ghetto, cut off from the rest of society and main taining contact mainly with one another. That selfsame society which only a little earlier had venerated them as its true spokesmen was, of course, well aware of their existence and sympathised with them, but at the same time took very good care to stay out of trouble, knowing full well that it was dangerous to have anything to do with the "outcasts" whose fate they could come to share if they did not watch out.

It was in this gloomy period that the idea of trying to escape from the closed world of writing "for the drawer" was born. Starting with a small circle of the most strictly "forbidden" authors (Kohout, Klíma, Kliment, Vaculík, myself, and a few others), these writers began to exchange their manuscripts with a view to copying them and circulating them to a wider readership. They started writing regular *feuilletons*, short literary essays which they sent to one another with the same intention. Others joined in and our pieces got around. A little later, things changed for the better, especially after—but to some extent already before—the birth of Charter 77, this Czech form of *samizdat* gaining unexpectedly wide currency. Today, there are a great many *samizdat* series circulating in Czechoslovakia, consisting of periodicals, individual articles and entire books, polemics, and various other texts, all this via a widespread network that has come about quite spontaneously, without any central organisation. Many of these articles and books find their way abroad and then return to our readers by courtesy of émigré publishers and Czech and Slovak broadcasting stations.

One of the members of that small, original circle was

Ludvík Vaculík, an experienced writer and journalist well known to our public from the days when he was still allowed to publish, not just for his novel *The Axe* but also for his brave journalistic activity in the 1960s—he was, for instance, the author of the famous *2,000 Words* manifesto in the spring of 1968. Unlike the rest of us, who used the *feuilleton* genre only occasionally, Vaculík with characteristic doggedness, has remained faithful to it and is to this day writing his three-page essays, putting one into circulation every month, regular as clockwork.

His highly individual way of thinking, his personal character and style, allied to his native stubbornness, have given rise to a unique phenomenon. Vaculík has originated his very own type of *feuilleton*, departing from the traditional form of the genre. Although on the surface they continue to be *called* feuilletons, his pieces have long since become something else, and something more: Vaculík has created a completely original form, in which his personal reflections, his views and experiences are fused with topical accounts and most skilfully reshaped into artistic ministructures whose effects far exceed the expectations we as readers have of the genre. Individual, seemingly quite unconnected themes are linked by a delicate and frequently surprising web of associations, thanks to which the essay (usually in its very last sentence) turns out to be an absolutely consistent whole, with nothing left to chance, no matter how this may have seemed to be the case. Its message comes over not only through its poetic effect but also—perhaps mainly—as a result of that peculiar view of the world that is typical of Vaculík. And there is something more: his inimitable idiom, his diction, his melody, his habit of wresting unexpected meanings from mundane associations, his irony and humour.

I bow in admiration before anyone who tries to translate Vaculík's *feuilletons* into another language, sharing the feelings of bitterness a translator will inevitably experience at the sad realisation that that which is most characteristically ''Vaculík'' defies translation.

Vaculík's *feuilletons* are today generally known and popular here in Czechoslovakia among all who take an interest in literature. The author's personality—stubborn, unconventional, somewhat morose, exceptionally sensitive and capable of soberly reflecting upon itself and its troubles—is now firmly established in Czech spiritual life of the second half of our century. I wait eagerly to see how this selection of his work will be received by the foreign reader. That is a question that concerns far more than just the author himself, his success—or lack of it—abroad. The question really is to what extent has contemporary Czechoslovakia, and contemporary Central Europe, been cut off from the rest of the world. Or, in other words, to what extent are we today still able to understand one another.

Free to Use a Typewriter

Preface to a "Padlock" collection of essays by several authors

In France last year they passed a law to protect their language against English. They even intend to set up committees and to punish offenders. France is sending back not only words like "snack-bar" and "play-back", but also "cameraman", "manager" and hundreds of others. During a parliamentary debate on the subject a Communist deputy said this was silly and that the French language had to be safeguarded differently: by safeguarding France.

How are we to protect the Czech language?

The difference in our case lies in that our language is being rotted from within, it is all due to rotten Czechs, if you like. They have a very limited vocabulary and almost unlimited scope for using it in public, a puny theme and a vast amount of patience in sticking to it, lean ideas and fat powers. These people have established something like a Basic Czech containing 850 words.

When did you last read anything interesting in the papers? By that I don't mean interesting reports about matters economic or technical, about natural phenomena or political revolutions, but an interesting *idea* on any of these subjects. You can progress along the road of discovery without anything really new being said, until such time as someone gets a personal feeling about it and tries to put his thoughts into words. It is only this need to express a new idea that disturbs the sediment of a language and stirs it up thoroughly, from the bottom. Ideas provide a language with inspiration, information exhausts it. The repetition of the same "information" over and over again literally stifles it. That is why I believe that it'll only be when the technicians and scientists have had their fill of space flights and, for once, give way to a poet or a witty woman from some agricultural cooperative that we shall at last hear something new about space. I, too, would like to go there.

The contributions which, in the course of the past year, have come together between these covers have not been commissioned by anyone, nobody paid any fees for them, edited or censored them. Nor am I now their editor, making my selection from among them. Here they all are, each and every one. Some serve as a record of their time, others help to redress the moral balance in the reader's mind, others still may at the very least entertain him and give him something else to think about.

It has to be said that in our country we enjoy a great deal of freedom to use a typewriter. Why, though, you may ask, could not these articles appear in the official press? No, there's nothing wrong with that—after all they don't express official sentiments or attitudes. Some of them, needless to say, have managed to stay within the bounds of legality only by a whisker. I don't mean to inform on myself or on anyone else, but I do think this is something of a failure. Why must we be eternally condemned to this system of confrontation? Surely a different system should be possible: a system of great variety. An unconventional theme. A high degree of sublimation of politics, as in the case of Pithart. Or why not write about something entirely different, as do Hruza and Kanturková. I would consider it a success if our imaginary censor had no comment to make about our *feuilletons,* because what we wrote simply did not remind him of anything, did not in any way concern him. Or, another possibility: if he felt some sympathy and was gradually won over.

I have been referring to the Czech language all the time, for I have nothing to say about Slovak. Everything's fine in Slovakia, I don't believe Kadlečik, because none of his fellow-countrymen confirms his feelings. And Šimečka isn't a Slovak. I suppose he has written about some of us in Slovak because he would have found it impossible to do so in Czech.*

20 April 1977

---

*Milan Šimečka, banned sociologist, author of the important *Restoration of Order* (1978), and Vaculík's friend, appears later in this collection in ''The Trail of the Lawman''.

My Philosophers

The Marxist philosopher Karel Kosík played an important role in the intellectual ferment which led to the abortive attempt to liberalise the Czechoslovak political system in 1968. After the Soviet invasion in August of that year he was prevented from working in his field and from publishing his work. In June 1976 Kosík celebrated his 50th birthday. His friend Vaculík marked the occasion with this tribute, which appeared in the "Padlock Editions".

Before Karel Kosík I have, since my childhood, not known any philosophers at first hand. For one thing, there were fewer of them in Brumov than in Prague, and in any case, some of them weren't even philosophers.

Take, for instance, Tonek, who was said to be a philosopher. Tonek was a man of indeterminate age and of no evident profession who used to walk around the village, stopping here and there to watch what others were doing, nod his head, and go off again somewhere else. I know neither who gave him food, nor where he lived, what his surname was, or which school he had been to. "He leads a simple life," people would say when he had left. "He has no underpants." I thought, naive as I was, that they were referring to his meagre apparel. Only now, as I write this, do I realise that they meant something else. Tonek looked well, a healthy face and, under his shirt which he wore open to the waist, a strong physique. He didn't drink, cause disturbances, steal or smoke. On Sunday mornings he would go and get a shave and trim; he could afford that, as he always managed to earn a few crowns during the week. From time to time he would arouse interest by having all his shirt and trouser buttons sewn on. "Just look at Tonek!" they would say approvingly in front of the grocer's, by the village pump, outside the smithy, and so on. And they would try and guess whose fair hand had done the sewing. Tonek would just smile and, using the fingers of both hands, run them along the buttons from top to bottom as if playing the clarinet, until finally he would tap his organ; a musician's custom.

Wherever Tonek went, he was asked the same question: "Tell us, Tonek, when are you going to get married?" Year after year, in winter or summer, Tonek replied in guttural tones: "Winter comes." His questioners shook their heads and said: "My, my, what a philosopher!" But he wasn't one. Or was he?

The second man whom, in my early pre-Kosík period, I took to be a philosopher was František Balej. I was sixteen when, using some of the well-earned money I received in wages from the Bata shoe factory in Zlín, I bought a second-hand book called *The Golden Pen* under the impression that it was a thriller. I was surprised by the seriousness of the text and delighted that I understood it. What an introduction to philosophy! The book contained an essay on mystery; there was, it said, a difference between the mysterious and the unknown—the unknown should be made known, that was why *Homo* was *sapiens*, but mysteries should remain, and any sensible man should respect that. Today we remember František Balej (1879-1918) as a translator of Tagore, and I am probably the only one to think of him as a philosopher. When I found the book again the other day and re-read it, I was surprised how simple and obvious were the ideas it contained. They were perhaps my oldest ideas. Question is, did I get them from Balej, or did he get them from me?

I have tried on various occasions to squeeze through the fence of philosophical parks. Once, I devoted a whole Sunday afternoon to this pursuit, having borrowed a copy of H.G. Wells' *History of the World*; and while the other boys from my dormitory went into town to enjoy themselves, I barked my shins, metaphorically speaking, on realism and nominalism, this couple of concepts in fact serving to bar my way forward for some time afterwards. I made yet another attempt with the aid of Emanuel Chalupný's slender volume called *The Logic of Science*, but that turned out to be about something else than I had hoped. I was almost eighteen and badly needed to know what philosophy was all about!

Slender volumes promise the simplest introduction, and that is why I avidly reached out for the booklet "On Dialectical and Historical Materialism" by J.V. Stalin, who also tinkered with philosophy. The lightning of perception illuminated my darkness. And it took some time before I was to realise the true nature of this effect: the sharp light simply dazzled the eye, suffusing all questions, yet when one shielded one's eyes from the glare, one could see the nests of one's old doubts. For instance: if everything was now so crystal-clear, why were there philosophers who clung to different views? Surely they have more gumption than that?

And so the man who came to have the most lasting influence on me was M.K. Gandhi (1869-1948). Non-violent civil disobedience which makes tyrants weep, now that's the thing. My head went round at the thought, I had to go and tell everybody about it. I even gave a lecture on the subject to my fellow-shoemakers. What I again failed to grasp was that I was once more not finding intercourse with the pure body of philosophy but rather with its crude application to the masses. And the masses going into action in the streets at the behest of a philosophy—we Europeans ought to know better by now. Nevertheless, I cannot help, time and again, feeling excited at the thought of a mass of people consisting of impenetrable individuals, each of whom acts with pride and purity, each in his own individual way, wittily, legally and, above all, unceasingly. No, this possibility has not been sufficiently investigated and tested in our country.

What's with my philosophy, then? I must confess that I didn't have one in my pre-Kosík era. True, I did arrive at a kind of cosmological-pragmatic system which allowed me to act while leaving difficult problems, like God, aside out of sheer incapability, until such a time as life or death would provide further guidance. I have no intention of elaborating on this system of mine, though, and especially not in writing. As soon as you set down cognition in writing, it ceases to be true, for the vectors of truth have changed.

There can be no fixed cognition, there is only an unbounded continuum of cognition, which keeps changing as it flows from mind to mind, and an uninterrupted continuum of subject and object. I am on the Earth → I am the Earth → I am the Sun ... There is thus no idealism or materialism, because there is no reason for them in the phenomena which they attempt to explain. But there are butterflies pinned down in a poisonous box.

Just think! Give the same piece of information to a number of thinkers, and what happens? Each of them will present you with a different philosophy, since each had a mother and she either breast-fed him or not. And then he was either allowed to go to London or not. Schools of philosophy and influences? Yes, but also stomachs (ability to conform to regimes), penises (ability to create alternatives to revolution) and, last but not least, patience. The philosophy of a bald philosopher will differ from that of a bearded one as does bread from different bakers, even though they use the same flour.

If anything, in my pre-Kosík period I tended to favour the philosophy of non-philosophers. Although I respect Marx and de Chardin, these gentlemen don't scare me. Havlíček and Neruda, for instance, do, they give me a feeling of inferiority. And I am most impressed, in a quite topical fashion, by men like Mayor Pštross (1823-63), or, in Slovakia, the lawyer M.Š. Daxner (1823-92).

Karel Kosík (1926-2026) is the first philosopher I have ever got to know in person. They showed him to me once at an editorial meeting at *Literární noviny*. He did not stand out either by reason of his size or his sonorous delivery;

his evident authority must have been due to his character, behaviour, opinions, or even his philosophy. He was the author of *Dialectics of the Concrete* and no doubt other things. I had not read a single line of his. We looked at one another, and I saw at once that he was favourably impressed, and therefore so was I. He took an approving view of my work, which pleased and encouraged me. He is a sound philosopher, that I can vouch for.

Karel Kosík (1926-2026) lives in an attic flat in Hradčany Square, access to which is gained by a winding iron staircase, like in an engine-room. The furnishings are sparse but utilitarian and tasteful. Kosík dresses inconspicuously to the point of nonchalance, but with care. He wears spectacles. In dealing with visitors he is mindful of the purpose of their visit, and of time. I should say he tends to observe rather than experience. He possesses a good, well-controlled sense of humour. Physically, too, he has all the necessary attributes of a philosopher, except maybe a certain lack of stamina in his backside. He speaks French and German, and I am sure also some Russian. In discussions it's his custom to speak last, after which it invariably seems that there is nothing more left to say. He is to be admired for his struggle with the rodent which has invaded his garden at Všenory. Use has been made of carbide, gas, poison, a whole bank has been dug over, and yet the rodent survives at Všenory, as does Kosík at Hradčany.

Karel Kosík (1926-2026) spends whole days writing his philosophy on a typewriter. Last year in April the State Security, in all its glory, took away the manuscript of his work to have it evaluated in the police philosophy shop.

Kosík complained to various quarters, including Sartre, and then he told me: "You know something? They actually helped me by taking that manuscript. I had to write it again and was able to see various things more clearly." When at last he won and had his philosophy returned, he read it through and said morosely: "It's not as good as I thought." None of us, his friends, is allowed to know what he's writing, not until it's finished, he says, and so only God and Lieutenant-Colonel Noga know. It goes without saying that, unless conditions improve, the book cannot possibly be published here, except in "Padlock", and if conditions deteriorate, then not even there. Kosík keeps postponing the deadline by which he is supposed to complete the manuscript and deliver it to his friends, so my pre-Kosík period keeps growing longer. Day before yesterday I asked him, perhaps for the twentieth time: "When are you going to finish it?" He shrugged his shoulders, and I prompted him: "Not till winter comes, I suppose?" He nodded and went off somewhere else.

This took place in Hradčany Square, where a few of us had met to discuss what to do in an important matter. Several useful suggestions were made, all of which were sensibly ruled out of court by Karel Kosík. We had to do it without him, weaker by one. On our way home, Ivan Klíma and I continued the conversation and we agreed that, unfortunate though it was, Kosík was probably right. Well, so be it.

There it was: how were we to act when the way things were we had to act before we could discover the way they were?—Now kindly read that sentence again and I'll demonstrate Kosík at work. After practically each word put a question mark: act?—were we?—have to—before?—we could?

I could not with impunity cross out any of those question marks. But if we then do nothing, what will happen to our moral—and humoral—fibre? That is the question—an ordinary, commonplace, undramatic, fateful, Czech question.

Had I not moved to Prague but stayed in the village where I was born, I could today have filled the empty post of the local philosopher, going my rounds of the village, nodding my head and occasionally playing the clarinet. I would have had it made.

11 June 1976

The Genie

Yesterday afternoon I went to the Slavia Café, hoping to find Jiří Kolář there and to give him the new typescript volume of Pavel Hruza's *Sounds of Silence*. Kolář wasn't there, but Karol Sidon got up from one of the tables and came to greet me. I had not seen him for a long time, he had not been one of those even who came to congratulate me on my birthday week before last. I realised this as we came towards each other, and wondered if Karol would realise it too. "When is that birthday of yours?" he asked as he shook my hand. "You've missed it, I'm afraid," I told him and asked whether our mutual friends had not wanted him to write something on my present. "Yes, they did," he replied, "but, to tell you the truth, I wasn't sure what to call you." "Why, just normally, whatever it is you do call me." "Well, maybe you haven't noticed, but I try to avoid that…" He was right, I hadn't noticed. Though of course I did realise long ago that he always used the formal mode of address when speaking to me, while I used the familiar *Ty*. Yet I suspected that if I suggested a change, he might regret doing it. Why should that be? Probably because he was just a boy when he started visiting us, and

I suppose he looked up to me. That's all of fifteen years ago. "But you know what you can still do? You can write a *feuilleton*—about anything you like." He promised to write one, but then he had done that twice before.

He took me to his table, where a friend of his and a girl were sitting. We chatted a while, and then I noticed a man at a table by the window, dark-skinned, thin and dry-looking, immaculately dressed, with a grey-coloured tie. He was middle-aged and looked ill and sad. We tried to guess his nationality, suggesting that he was a Rumanian, Hungarian, a Slovak Hungarian, definitely a Southerner. He was sitting there on his own, with just a pack of cigarettes and his lighter on the table in front of him. All of a sudden he rose, crossed over to us, and said in English: "You're talking about me." "Yes, we are," I replied, also in English. "You're trying to guess my nationality." "Yes, we are," I said again. "Well, tell me, what nationality am I?" "Rumanian or Hungarian." But no, he was an Arab. "Where from?" I asked. "From Baghdad," he replied. "That's the city of Sindbad the Sailor," I said. "Do you know the fairy-tale?" "Yes, of course," he said, looking pleased. "But it's thirty years since I read that story." I had to test him, to see if he really did come from Baghdad. 'What does *Alph laila va-laila* mean?" I asked him. "That is a thousand nights and one night in Arabic," he said. "Right you are," I said, and asked him how long he was in Prague for, and what he was doing here. He replied that where he came from it was too hot. He had been in Prague a month now, and it was his second time in two years as a tourist. Before that, he had been in Salonika and Athens, but Prague was nicer. Then he asked me if I knew the story about the genie in the bottle. I said everyone knew that story, and Karol agreed, as did his friend, only the girl didn't say anything because she had a swathe of black hair hanging across her lips, through which she just about managed to stick her cigarette.

I asked the man from Baghdad what their genie was doing, these days. He said he wasn't sure but he thought he was back in his bottle. I said they should take good care. Our genie had escaped and we could not get him back. He asked when did we release him. I explained, and then I asked him whether he knew how to get the genie back into his bottle. "Ah," he said, laughing, "if only I knew that, I'd have lots of money."

Karol suggested I ask the man from Baghdad why he liked it here better than in Greece. He hesitated before replying, looked slowly around the room and out at the busy street with the view of the National Theatre and the bridge over the Vltava. "There's more freedom here." For a moment there was a stunned silence, then Karol's friend, who probably meant to say simply that it wasn't true, said, even better: "Oh no, this isn't real!"

I had to leave just then, as I was meeting Ivan [Klíma] in Hradčany Square. He was already there, waiting for me, he and Pavel. "I've just given Pavel my finished novel to read," he said, nudging me with his shoulder, adding: "A thousand pages, but it's fine." Wait a minute, I said to myself, what if he's right—but I liked to hear him boast like that. Pavel explained how badly his application for a trip to the USA was progressing, and Ivan said that he would similarly not be going to Sweden. He started telling us about a visit he had had from Mr Obrda, who had come to tell him that, following our recent visit to Mr Václav [Havel] in his country retreat at Hrádeček, he had been interrogated by the secret police, who wanted to know what had transpired. I must point out here that Mr Obrda could not tell them anything as we didn't trust him, he had turned up out of the blue and uninvited; but I hate saying this about him, because he cooks so well. We mulled it around for a bit, and then decided: "Either this Obrda is lying, or they know nothing." But all three of us thought *that* was impossible.

At that moment Kosík and Bartošek stopped for a minute by our bench, and then went on. Then Rudolf Slánský Jr drove past, waving a greeting. "I don't believe this," said Pavel, laughing. "In the end they'll have to put a bug into one of these statues." "I have just been talking to an Arab," I said, "who thinks there's more freedom here than in Greece." My two friends did not say anything for a while, ruminating on my Arab piece of nonsense. Finally, even without Kosík, they came to the conclusion that there was no accounting for taste.

But seriously, what if the man from Baghdad was right? What if he, sitting lonely in a coffee-house in Athens and then in Prague, gazing out of the window and watching the people go by, trying to read their conversations from their lips—what if he were able to glean more than a garrulous journalist who comes here at convenient intervals and with his mind made up, looking for confirmation of his views and always to the same people? The man from

Baghdad, with no mission to fulfil and a completely different *modus operandi*, may well be better able to assess his surroundings, gauge the atmosphere of a place and ascertain with what degree of inborn freedom people behave and interact. Human freedom, which I am sure is a much wider concept than so-called political freedom, develops together with the inhabitants under weightier pressures than flash-in-the-pan regimes lasting half a century. It has nothing to do with the openness of a political system, or its opposite—indeed, it seems to me that perhaps this type of freedom thrives more in places which have strict regimes than in the very free ones, where the *need* for freedom is not so acutely felt and where people, so many of them, don't have to reflect daily on how to define it. The genie can only hover above all this as if he were floating above the sand dunes of the desert, but he cannot change the nature of the sand.

I came home to find a letter from Milan Šimečka in Bratislava waiting for me. In it he mentioned our visit to Hrádeček, saying how pleasant it was. "This," he wrote, "was no doubt suspected by our comrades, the Majors, and I had no sooner returned home than here they were, urging me to tell them how we had enjoyed it."

And today I received a nice *feuilleton* from Milan Uhde in Brno, about the satirist Karel Havlíček Borovský. At the end of his typewritten letter, Milan had added by hand: "On Wednesday, on my return from Hrádeček, we had a half-day social—otherwise no news."

Oh well, so what. Next year, if Mr Václav decides to ask us we'll all come again.

3 August 1976

May Day

It was the first of May...

"Forgive me"—wrote Jan Neruda in 1890—"if I, too,
begin with this charming poetic phrase of ours which, nevertheless, these days sounds dangerously like a cliché..."

And so please forgive *me*, that, in this year of 1975, I
choose, a little naively perhaps, to hide behind Neruda here
on the Letná Plain so as to give vent to my own feelings
about May Day—or, more accurately, about the sum total
of all the May Days which come to mind when I reflect
on everything that has happened in the eighty-five years
since Neruda wrote:

What a strange day! A strange mood! No, not fear—
oh, no, nothing like that—but a strange expectancy,
waiting for something vague and quite unknown, which
set all my nerves tingling. Not a pleasant feeling. I
remember only two other occasions in my life when
(though there really is no similarity whatever with this
third such moment) I felt just like that...The first time
was in 1848, during the bombardment of Prague; I was
aware of exactly the same sort of feeling as I listened to
the sound of mortars going off at intervals. And the

second time in 1866, that morning when the Prussians were approaching Prague.

Today, it is a risky business just to copy that paragraph, which Neruda wrote quite freely all those eighty-five years ago: comparing his feelings as he waited for the workers' march to pass by (an event he was in sympathy with) with those he experienced on two catastrophic occasions. Well, that is quite a well-known phenomenon—we may well feel the same tingling sensation when witnessing some great and good event as when we are afraid, and, vice versa, some great and evil happening, such as for example a natural catastrophe, can evoke feelings that may be described as aesthetic. An idiot, however, would then, too, have plagued Neruda with questions: "What put you in mind of a bombardment, of all things?" "And what did you mean by 'the Prussians?' " —The only thing is, in those days the idiot didn't have official sanction to ask those questions.

But of course, I too had no reason to fear that multitude on Letná Plain. On the contrary, I felt more protected here than in my own home, which only a few days earlier had been ransacked during a police search. The depressed feeling I had been conscious of ever since then, whether sitting at home or wherever I went outside, here seemed to lift, as if it were scraped off as I pushed through the crowd. They all looked the same, adopting a protective uniformity. I had decided, just for fun, to try and tell how many workers and foremen were here, how many white-collar workers and their bosses. Well, it turned out to be an impossible task: maybe this particular celebration had selected all these look-alikes regardless of profession and social origin, but

on the other hand we all know that we don't, in this country, have any particularly sharp class distinctions. "Annie,
love, come with me into the woods..." the sound of the
brass band came loud and clear from the many
loudspeakers, just like at a fair, and I suddenly felt light
and free of care, as if I were walking past the swings and
merry-go-rounds. Yet, at the same time I was conscious
of a sadness at my defeat—it seemed wrong to get rid of
fear in this devious way.

Huge grey balloons floated above the Plain, each Prague
district having its own, with the number marked on it. The
people were criss-crossing the open space, making for their
particular number. White lines had been painted on the
ground, leading from these balloons, with members of the
Workers Militia lined up on them wearing uniforms of
military material and cut but overall-blue in colour. Their
commanding officers communicated with each other by
means of walkie-talkies. Stewards wearing armbands
showed people to their places, so that no-one who had
decided to turn out today could possibly get lost. Once safely
in their allotted space, it was an easy matter to find their
own factory or firm, designated by a large sign, or their
foremen or bosses, who had come earlier. A man with a
child sitting astride his shoulders, who had just found his
place in the crowd, cracked a joke: "Here I am, Mr
Svoboda, be sure to tick my name off!"

A cool breeze drove low clouds scudding across the sky,
fluttering the banners carried by selected individuals and
the flags on their poles above the as yet empty podium at
the top end of Letná Plain. There was about half an hour

to go. The crowd milled around me, and I reflected on it. Neruda writes about the "menacing silence" of the marching workers, guided by an idea whose power "altered the entire social and political situation at one fell swoop".

I cannot help but think that, since those days at the end of the last century, the workers must have achieved what they wanted, since they were so placid, no longer menacing but chatting away in friendly fashion about the things they have and not a word about any changes which would bring them more... (Someone rings my doorbell, so I quickly remove the paper from my typewriter and hide it before going to open the door. It was the rent collector. What a pleasant surprise!)

The rhythmical pounding of the marching music suddenly stops and the loudspeakers relay our National Anthem: *Where Is My Home* and *Lightning Over the Tatras*. We all stand to attention, even the children who cannot resist quietly digging into the sand with the heels of their shoes. On the podium, draped in revolutionary red, I can now see the black Sunday-best suits of the workers' representatives, the gleaming spectacles of government ministers, several arms raised in salute with fingers pointed at a general's hat. The revolutionary flags snap gently in the May breeze. Like forked lightning, a thought strikes me that makes me recall the Paris Commune, the red flags of the anarchists...

"What a strange day!" I distinctly hear Jan Neruda whisper, standing there forgotten on the pavement at Příkopy. He of course couldn't know that the route of the march had long ago changed (not like in his day, just from

Karlín to Střelecký ostrov), and so the workers' battalions had passed by and their leaders, having boarded official limousines en route, had now reached the Letná Plain.

The anthem was over. And then, as the leading workers' leader, Dr Gustav Husák, stepped up to the mike in order to speak about the common weal, something quite unexpected happened: I could not hear a thing. The assembled populace was again loudly discussing their daily achievements, their entertainments, children, and the weather. I stayed on for a while, and then started for home, my mind in a whirl.

Yes: it was the first of May 1975!

"And whichever mature and thinking man was there to witness it, will not forget it to the end of his days."

7 May 1975

Good News?

I find I have a shortage of good news. Yes, I know, I'm
not alone. (There, another piece of bad news.) I can hardly
remember when something happened to give me a pleasant
surprise. And it has been years since I last received a
favourable official communication. Whenever I receive a
letter in an official envelope, I know that this or that application of mine has again been turned down. I have a whole
pile of unopened letters containing this kind of news. The
arrival of such a letter now invariably causes my stomach
to contract and I involuntarily hunch my shoulders. It has
become a *tic*, but one that the authorities are also suffering
from, don't you think? Yes, I'm sure they are.

Looking at it another way, you could say that there is
something quite special about someone getting nothing but
unfavourable replies from his native authorities. There must
be some good reason for this, some definite purpose behind
it. The whole thing has acquired a certain style, it is not
without a certain pathos and humour. You might almost
consider it an *oeuvre*. I would therefore be disappointed if,
just as the tenth anniversary of this state of affairs
approaches, someone were deliberately to spoil it by respon-

ding favourably to some trifling request of mine. No, not that! Either provide me with a clean run of good news—or nothing.

And yet, if we are to keep our mental health we do need the occasional good piece of news, no matter how insignificant. This universal need gives rise, from time to time, to anonymously disseminated joyful tidings, but these no one believes any longer, we have all discovered that an isolated item of exaggeratedly good news cannot possibly be true. It's the same as with mushrooms: they either grow or they don't, and the odd one merely deprives the mushroom enthusiast of time and energy.

Letters from friends constitute a quite special source of news. The very fact that a friend has chosen to write to me is good news; and so is the fact that the letter has actually reached me. However, the contents of the letter, even if it is favourable, cannot signify too much. Unless there is a general improvement in the kitchen where the raw material for our news is processed, not even good news sent by our friends can mean all that much. Here is an example: My friend Milan Uhde has written to me from Brno. Good news, that. He wrote to say that the State Literary Agency, Dilia, has forwarded to him an author's fee from France in the sum of 56 crowns. Well, the uninitiated might say, that too is good news. But the expert would want to know what rate of exchange Dilia has used to calculate the conversion, whether the normal rate or the discriminatory one. At the same time, they sent him an invoice for the payment of 11 crowns, this being the requisite tax.

So what is friend Uhde actually telling me? A moment's

thought will show me that it would really have been better if Dilia had not sent him anything. "No news is good news" I was taught (in English) when I attended business school, though not of course in the commercial correspondence class.

Or, again, a letter from Václav Havel. Letters from Mr Václav are always good news, if for no other reason than because of the bright felt pens he uses to highlight the most important passages and to sign his letters. This time he wrote to announce the glad tidings that he would take me in his car to the PEN Congress in Vienna. He concluded with the favourable news that, as I no doubt knew (I didn't!), we would probably not have to pay for the trip ourselves, as the organisers realised that we could not do so. All this, conveyed in a well-nigh childlike, joyful tone, in a private letter cannot but delight the recipient. But I, God help me, kept the whole thing secret, pretending that I knew nothing about any PEN Congress, much less that anyone would want to invite us to take part in it. Such things I no longer mention even in the privacy of my home, and I would therefore not dream of blabbing about it in letters to friends, for our inquisitive authorities to read. So is it still a piece of good news? By return of post I attempted to cover up Mr Václav's revelation by saying that I accepted his invitation to give me a lift in his car, but that we would go to the devil, not to Vienna. In order not to dismay him, I hinted—in a way that he but no one else would understand—that just before we got there, we might possibly change course and make for a more pleasant destination. A coded message, so to speak.

Now I'm on tenterhooks whether I'll really get that invitation to Vienna. Although I don't actually know if that would be a good piece of news or not. For, if I *were* invited, I'd have to apply for a passport. And what if I got it? Then I would really be in a fix.

All I want is peace and quiet, and nothing else. No news is good news—for the time being.

A fortnight ago I asked one of my friends to buy me in the town he lives in something that I cannot obtain in Prague: an assortment of rasps for filing wood of various sizes and thicknesses, and two carpenters' clamps. I would send the money by return. Today I received a parcel. Its shape told me at once that it did not contain the clamps. What it did contain were six identical rasps and 20 identical wooden handles for them. I was flabbergasted—what use were six rasps, one exactly like the other? I wouldn't need that many for the rest of my life. And what was he sending me 20 handles for, was he nuts, or couldn't he read? A bad piece of news, or a bad joke that I would have to pay for.

There was a letter inside the parcel. My friend wrote to say that not even in their town could he find what I needed. Just to please me, he was at least sending me the tools he had been able to sign out in the store at the factory where he worked, and there was nothing to pay. As a piece of good news this hardly gets off the ground—my friend, who obtained the rasps for his own work, used to be a university professor.

22 September 1975

A Cup of Coffee with My Interrogator

Unless you have been through it yourself, you wouldn't believe how difficult it is to avoid replying to polite questions. Not only does it go against the grain not to reply, because of one's good upbringing, but it is also difficult to keep up because it is hard on the ears. A beginner finds it next to impossible. Worst of all, it doesn't make for good relations between the parties concerned, the rift thus created being often insurmountable. Which is what I mean to write about.

Undeterred by his lack of success, Lieut-Colonel Noga began anew each morning: "Would you please get your papers ready, Blanička." His secretary, Blanka, took out a clean sheet of paper, carbons and flimsies, put them in her typewriter and, fingers poised above the keyboard, turned her face towards her boss. He hesitated while he thought out his question, then he asked me, "Would you care for a cup of coffee?" I decided to accept the coffee.

Lieut-Colonel Noga is a smallish man, well built, dark of skin and hair. Originally a factory worker, his behaviour and speech indicate that he has spent many years in a different environment. His Czech is correct, but there is

something about his pronunciation which hints at another Slav language. This wretched detail made me, willy nilly, adopt a kind of coquetry one tends to employ when dealing with fellow-countrymen.*

"All right, Mr Vaculík, you insist that your conduct isn't in breach of the law. Let's just suppose you're right," he was fond of saying. Then he would add, "Well then, why don't you tell me about it."

"I'm sorry, Lieut-Colonel," I would reply, "but I really don't feel I want to go over all that again."

"You don't feel you want to? What kind of talk is that? Why don't you say exactly what you mean—after all, this is your protocol: 'I refuse to testify!' "

Mrs Blanka looked up at me, I nodded shamefacedly, and she typed the words.

"When will you return my things to me?" I asked, pointing at the two suitcases standing beside his desk.

"Don't confuse the issue. Next question—take this down, Blanička: What is your opinion...of the way the Western press...is misusing the whole affair...for its slanderous campaign against Czechoslovakia?"

I dictated my reply: "I will answer this question as soon as I have had an opportunity to read what the Western press has to say on the subject."

"You so-and-so!" he rebuked me in mock anger, left the room and came back with a whole pile of foreign newspapers, which he slammed on the desk in front of me.

I requested Mrs Blanka to record: "When I say I want

* Like Vaculík himself, the interrogator comes from Moravia.

to read foreign newspapers, I mean when I can buy them at a news stand.''

In the course of that week of interrogations I was able to put any number of such impertinences into my statement. No one objected.

One evening there were just the two of us, as Mrs Blanka went home at four. He sat down on her stool, turned the roller in the typewriter, and said, ''Here we've been at it all day and we've got just seven pages. Not very much, is it?''

''There isn't going to be any more,'' I replied.

''Oh really? There is, you know.''

''All right, tell me something about nocturnal interrogation.''

He cast an alarmed eye at his watch. ''Half past seven already! But that still doesn't make it night.''

''Either have me put in a cell or send me home. But first of all, take me to the toilet.''

''Oh no, we don't lock up witnesses. I will take you to the toilet, though. Have you got some paper?''

I hadn't any, and so he picked up two clean sheets, crumpled them obligingly and handed them to me. Then he waited outside the toilet. Seeing that we had been at it all day, those two sheets were scarcely sufficient. Already on the second day it was clear to me that it was more of a siege than an interrogation. Once I had repeated my initial refusal, there was really nothing else for us to do. My Lieut-Colonel was in the habit of leaving the room for long periods at a time. As for Mrs Blanka, she found me a dreadful bore. On the first few days she tried to win me over.

"Why don't you want to testify? No one's punished for expressing his opinions. You ought to hear how we complain about the office canteen!"

"Yes, but just imagine that one day the canteen manager is given powers to have you all locked up."

"Oh, but that's absurd!"

"Isn't it. And then imagine it happening on a nationwide scale."

She shook her head at this, smiling like one who is amazed at a child's foolishness. Then she said, "Here the law is being respected, you know. For instance, the prisoners have a right to exercise, and look!" She beckoned me to the window.

She was speaking the gospel truth: down there in the courtyard, in deep, concrete pens, I could see the prisoners, dressed in brown, circling round, talking and laughing.

Every lunchtime Lieut-Colonel Noga escorted me to a little waiting-room, furnished something like a club. There I would be given frankfurters. On my way I would encounter Václav Havel or Professor Patočka. Most of all, however, I bumped into Dr Jiří Hájek. A friendly young woman always asked us, in Slovak: "Would you like a coffee after lunch?" A pleasant interlude.

"Today," said Dr Hájek, "I gave them a little lecture on why I thought the demand for Czechoslovakia's neutrality in August sixty-eight was a mistake."

I was surprised. "Do you mean to say you were *against* neutrality?"

It was his turn to be surprised. "So you also thought I advocated it?"

"Everyone thinks so," I told him. "Why, only yesterday they were saying as much on TV."

"But it simply isn't true," he said, and, with all the patience of thin men who wear thick-lensed glasses, gave me a little lecture on why he thought the demand for Czechoslovakia's neutrality in August sixty-eight had been a mistake.

Once Mrs Blanka had to leave us in order to have her flu injection, and the Lieut-Colonel and I were left on our own. He paced up and down the office, his hands behind his back, and I knew he was about to say something.

"Now the girl's gone, I'll tell you something man to man." I pricked up my ears. "Modern medicine, that is, psychology and sexology ..." a few more paces, "are agreed in the view ..." a few more paces, "that where a man and a woman are concerned ..." he stopped abruptly in front of me, "anything goes."

"Mm," I thought cautiously. He gave me a smile and wagged a good-humoured finger at me. "But you, you really deserve a thrashing."

In these circumstances it is best to keep quiet and try to divine what the man is leading up to. I am afraid I failed to divine it.

He took two red apples from his briefcase and gave me one. I asked what sort it was, and he told me, but I have since forgotten. What interested me was that the apples came from a tree that was only five years old and he had several kilos of them. And I was touched by his giving me one. So I told him what sort of apple trees I had out at Dobřichovice. "If I have to come back here again," I said, "and if I'm allowed to go there on Sunday, I'll bring you some."

"Why shouldn't you be allowed?" he asked.

Next day, instead of my briefcase I took a big shopping bag and filled it with everything I had heard a detainee ought to have.

"You've brought a different bag," he said at once.

"That's right. Today I either leave here a free citizen who doesn't get hauled in every day, or you must allocate me a cell."

He was taken aback. "Why, has anything happened?"

"I'll tell you what's happened. Here you are politeness itself, and out there in the street brutalities are taking place. Do you know what's happened to the Kohouts?"*

"I've heard something ..."

"And so you can keep your politeness. And let me tell you something I haven't told you before: when they brought me in for the first time, Martinovský told me I was under arrest, took away my house keys and said they were going to carry out a search. What can you tell me about that?"

"He said you were under arrest and took your keys?"

"That's right."

"Well, I wouldn't consider that proper."

"In that case, give me back my things."

He sat down behind his desk, saying nothing and with an annoyed expression on his face. Mrs Blanka looked shat-

---

* The playwright, Pavel Kohout, and his wife were manhandled by police when picked up for questioning in connection with Charter 77.

tered. Then Lieut-Colonel Noga said:

"Do you want coffee?"

"No, I don't," I replied.

I no longer remember what we put down in my statement that morning. At noon he wanted to take me to lunch as usual. I refused. He inclined his head to one side dispiritedly and said, "You are really angry, aren't you? But why are you angry with me? Have I not shown good faith?"

"No, you haven't. If you had, you would at least have returned my manuscripts."

His brow furrowed, he dashed out of the office, returned and threw a file in black cardboard covers on the desk. "There! But now you will go to lunch?"

A crisp winter afternoon was advancing behind the bars from the White Mountain towards the darkness. My Lieut-Colonel was standing by the window, his hands behind his back. From the courtyard came the sound of women's voices as female prisoners took their exercise.

"Look, Mr Vaculík," he said with a smile I could not see from where I was sitting, "I know you'll put all this into one of your articles..."

"I expect so, if I'm given half a chance."

He was silent for a while. Then:

"And you'll call it: 'A Cup of Coffee with the Interrogator' ".

I almost fell off the chair. It was no use—they knew everything.

The next day—it was a Friday—I had a pleasant surprise: they returned 53 volumes of "Padlock Publications".

I couldn't get them all into the suitcase. Lieut-Colonel Noga brought me a box, himself packed the books into it, tied it up and even made a little loop for me to carry it by.

"There, I've wrapped them up for you so nicely that I almost regret it."

On Sunday I went to Dobřichovice for the apples. And that evening, when I was beginning to think they wouldn't come, they did arrive with yet another summons, and I prepared a paper bag with samples of four different sorts of apple...

But on Monday, what a change! Well, so be it.

"Sit down," he said coldly. Mrs Blanka had her typewriter all ready and she, too, looked as if she didn't know me. My Lieut-Colonel thought for a bit and then said. "Have you changed your attitude over the weekend?"

I haven't, I thought, but *you* have. "No," I said out loud.

"And do you know how the workers are reacting?"

"Yes, I do."

"What if I were to put you in a car and take you to a factory and ask you to defend what you have written in front of the workers?"

"First of all I'd ask them if they had actually read what we have written."

He got up and hurried out of the room.

Now he's going to find me some workers, I thought.

He returned to his desk.

"Want some coffee?" he asked.

I didn't feel like coffee. "Yes," I replied.

Again he dashed out, maybe just to order the coffee, but he was gone for a suspiciously long time. Everything suddenly seemed suspicious to me, including the fact that they had returned those books. Mrs Blanka sat in silence. From the courtyard came the sound of men's voices, occasional laughter. I listened hard, trying to discern if Jiří Lederer was perhaps laughing down there now, or František Pavlíček or Václav Havel.*

No, I said to myself in sudden resolve. Chickenshit!

He came back, sat down at his desk and snapped at me: "Do you know Jiří Lederer?"

"Yes."

"Did you give him your articles to send abroad?"

"Look, Lieutenant-Colonel, let's be clear about this: you've been on about these articles of mine for two years now. Are they criminal? If not, it can't be a criminal offence to send them abroad either. I'm telling you this off the record. For the protocol, all I'm willing to say is: I refuse to testify."

Lunch. Jiří Hájek was already there when I arrived. We ate our frankfurters. "Would you like a coffee?" Jiří Hájek thanked her and said, "You're looking after us so well that we'll grow fat in here and then won't be able to get out between the bars, and you'll say it's all our own fault."

The girl laughed. "Oh dear me, no!"

In the elevator, as the Lieut-Colonel escorted me towards

* Jiří Lederer, a journalist, and the playwrights František Pavlíček and Václav Havel (together with stage director Ota Ornest) were arrested in January 1977. Havel, as well as Dr Jiří Hájek and the late Professor Jan Patočka, acted as a spokeman for the Charter. Professor Patočka died on 13 March, 1977 following police interrogation, while Dr Hájek, who was Minister of Foreign Affairs at the time of the 1968 invasion, is under constant surveillance.

the exit, I still debated with myself about those apples in the paper bag. But I stuck to my resolve: No. Chicken-shit! Perhaps it was hard of me, but it was just.

20 January 1977
(Copy to Lieut-Colonel Noga)

Fatal Illness

Professor P. died of a fatal illness. No, I'm not referring to the flu epidemic that swept Prague this winter and which the professor may have treated too casually, leaving his bed too soon. That he would have survived. Nor was it his heart disease, which he was familiar with and knew how to handle. A little rest, and he would have lived. Nor yet did he die of the brain haemorrhage that actually caused his death. That didn't have to, shouldn't have happened. So what *did* Professor P. die of?

Professor P. was a tall, well-built man. His face had the features of a tough, bony peasant, but his eyes were soft, his way of speaking slow and deliberate, for he always tried to express himself with precision. When posing questions he would frequently end the sentence with a temperamental full stop, showing his deep conviction. He had lived all his life in semi-seclusion, known only to his students, friends, and an intimate circle of philosophers. I can say little about his philosophy, which is too complicated for me. All I know is that it had to do, on the one hand, with Husserl and phenomenology—but, again, I don't know what *that* is— and, on the other, with the more comprehensible ideas of

Comenius and Masaryk. He also wrote articles and studies on topical subjects, commenting on what went on in our society, thereby giving food for thought to a much wider audience. Alas, we couldn't read his stuff very often, as he had trouble getting published. Occasionally he wrote for publication abroad, or using a pen name. Out of the thirty years of his pedagogical activity, he was only allowed to lecture publicly for about five, being appointed professor at Charles University twenty years after he was put forward for a professorship. Last June he was seventy years old.

Early this year Professor Jan Patočka's name went round the world when he became one of the spokesmen of Charter 77. And we all stood amazed at hearing him speak: the language he brought with him from his silent political life was quite different from that we were used to hearing from our better (or improved) officials. It was full of fresh arguments deriving from long-forgotten sources: pure logic, healthy common sense, personal experience and a feeling of good will towards one's opponents. The powers-that-be were here being addressed by someone with whom they had long since forgotten how to talk in an intelligent fashion, which is why they entrusted the word to newspaper ruffians, liars and thugs.

Had he stuck to his non-state philosophy, Professor Patočka could have continued his modest existence to a ripe old age. He could have carried on debating in the private circle of his young students and his growing number of devotees, signing the typescript ''Padlock Editions'' of his latest works, which could not be published officially. The philosopher Patočka did himself harm by daring to speak out as a citizen, whom for almost all his life no one had allowed to speak, so that at last he decided to stand up and be counted. In his last few articles, written in defence of Charter 77, he said in his quiet, decent, tolerant way, that we all wish to be equal before the law, which is what the law itself stipulates, but also in other ways: equal in having the natural right to differ. We not only have a right to freedom, we also have the heavy responsibility of freedom and discipline.

For older people this kind of talk was a reminder of that time of hope when Czech thinking independently looked at the ideals of socialism, before this became forbidden. For younger generations his words came as something quite unheard of and highly exciting. But where our rulers were concerned, it was intolerable. And so none of them listened—except one minister, but he was Dutch.

I was present when Professor Patočka got ready to meet Herr van der Stoel. I was surprised how quickly he changed out of his green dressing-gown into his Sunday best: dark suit, white shirt, tie, and above them his ruddy, energetic, and in the past few weeks perceptibly younger face. "But, Professor, you're still ill," I warned him. That was the last time I saw Professor Patočka. The next few days of his life were stolen by the police, who kept interrogating him. During the last interrogation he complained of feeling sick and asked to be allowed to go home. The interrogators were themselves worried about his condition, but they apologised, saying they lacked the authority to let him go. It was only when he became very ill that they phoned someone higher up and received permission to free him. Next day Professor

Patočka had to be taken to hospital, where he died a few days later by way of a brain haemorrhage from the fatal disease of civil liberty, respect for the law and statesman-like wisdom in this dear socialist Czechoslovakia of ours.

He died, a Czech in Europe. There can be no doubt that had he not stood up for his convictions he need not have died. After all, the rest of us also have a choice. If we continue to stand up for our convictions, we too can die like this. Such a death conveys the definitive NO when we want finally to be believed that we mean NO! If it in the end has to come to that, all I can say is that we shan't be the last in Europe to meet such a fate.

16 March 1977

Funeral of a Spokesman

I had intended to go to the funeral, but, as luck would have it, I received a summons to a certain official institution for exactly the same hour. What a coincidence, I thought, and wrote an apology to the said institution, giving the funeral as the reason why I could not come. Apart from this, I decided to play it smart. The funeral was to be at ten, so I left the house at six. But the official institution proved smarter: as I left the house at that incredibly early hour, I found a car waiting for me outside: a Tatra 603, that familiar, repugnant shape and sinister black colour.

When we reached our destination they took me to a room on the ground floor, where I was welcomed by two gentlemen, one about my age whose name I have forgotten, the other very young, who was called Kučera (his name was on the summons). The older man said:

"We've asked you to come because of the funeral. Don't worry, we aren't going to be nasty to you, we shan't even talk about the Charter, indeed, we don't have to talk at all, if you prefer. You can read if you have got something to read, if not we can lend you something. Or you can have a snooze. When the funeral's over, we'll send you home again. Have a seat." And he pointed to a chair by the window, while he sat on the other one, indicating to the younger man that he should sit behind the desk. "Why don't you do some studying," he suggested in a fatherly tone.

I laid aside my black overcoat, took out the paperback I had brought to read on the tram, and sat down. "Tell me," I asked, "what if I had stayed at home and not gone either to you or the funeral?"

"Why, we should've thought you were just resting, that's all."

"I see. Why then couldn't we have talked it over and come to some agreement?"

"Yes, why not," he replied cautiously. "Well, maybe next time..." he added with a smile.

He was a pleasant-looking fellow of about fifty, most likely an economist or technician, I surmised. He was not wearing the usual disguise of Mr Average, on the contrary, his clothes testified to a well-developed, personal taste. He could have been a member of the crime squad, a real detective, specially assigned to duty this day—after all, this was no ordinary funeral. He had been born in southern Bohemia, his father was a forestry worker. He had spent a modest but evidently happy childhood in the great outdoors, communing with trees and animals, sharing adventures and playing games with his friends of both Czech and German nationality. Then something happened that divided them. Czechoslovak soldiers arrived in the forest and occupied the concrete bunkers. His father was called up for military service. The soldiers and the Czech inhabitants were eager to fight and defend their country.

One morning their teacher came into the classroom, the pupils stood up, the teacher looked at them silently for a while, and then said: "So we no longer have a Republic." And he burst into tears. The frontier regions were occupied by the Wehrmacht, he and his family joined the other Czechs in their evacuation to the interior... this and all that followed "these youngsters have only heard about in history classes", he concluded, indicating the young man behind the huge desk. "You studying?" he asked, opening a copy of *Rudé právo*, the Party daily.

I opened my book. It was half past seven.

"What's that you're reading?" he asked me.

"*What We're Like* by Ferdinand Peroutka," I replied, not intending to discuss the book with them. But when I saw the young man raise his head and look towards me with interest, I changed my mind. "It's a book of reflections on the character of the Czech nation, written in 1920. Peroutka questions whether the characteristics usually ascribed to us are really true. For instance, whether we are a humane nation, peaceloving or aggressive, to what extent we believe in democracy, need freedom, are capable of discipline, how diligent are we, and so on."

"Is that so?" said the man. The younger one returned to his studies. From the street outside the window came the voices of the drivers chatting as they waited at the wheels of their cars. "You seen Jarda anywhere? If you see him, tell him from me..."

And I went on reading:

"If you wish to discover what we Czechs really believe in, you will find that, first and foremost, we believe that people should live well and be happy. That is what all modern nations profess, and no 'Slav virtues' can alter that. Understanding this is a key to understanding the motivation behind our new political life.''

Somewhat surprisingly under the circumstances, I read with real concentration, occasionally marking a sentence on the page. I realised that I was taking in what I read more quickly than usual. The knowledge that there was nothing else to be done anyway and that I had a set time in which to do my reading undisturbed brought back long-forgotten feelings of satisfaction at hours spent in profitable study. Why didn't I arrange it so I could do this *every* morning of my own accord? This book in my hands, these two people here in the room with me, this building with all its sounds and imagined goings-on, the voices and footsteps outside, just beyond the window, my awareness of the forthcoming main event of the day, my experience of the last few years and of the more lively last few weeks—was all this not absolutely splendid, you might almost say scientific material for a study on the given theme of ''What We're Like?''

From outside came the sudden sound of many fat car doors banging shut, of many cars quietly starting up and quickly driving off—then silence. I gave a jump—at this rate I'm going to miss the funeral! It was half past nine. My contemporary also looked at his watch, although he could have asked me the time. Folding his newspaper, he took a magazine from his briefcase and started doing a crossword.

''Masaryk's Czech ideals are more or less universal

human ideals. Masaryk may see the courage to think for oneself, consistency in life, humaneness and a determined stand against evil and violence as Czech characteristics,'' writes Peroutka, ''but I have to say that there is no nation so wretched that it would not be capable of aspiring to the same ideals.'' I recalled that Jaspers, too, dealing with what was alleged to be the German national character, says that it is but an abstraction and that we should be looking at a nation's geographical position rather than at this imaginary ''national character''. In other words, if you transferred the English nation to Germany, Englishmen would behave like Germans, says Jaspers, or perhaps this was only my interpretation of what he was saying. However that may be, the fact is that ever since then I had found a certain consolation in these words. On occasion this has even helped me to stand up to Western journalists, with their nonchalant, offensive compassion for us, or again their cheap arrogance born of safety and well-being.

On the other hand Patočka—I glanced at my watch and laid aside the book—somewhere quotes Herder (only I cannot remember whether to agree with him or not), who was of the opinion that the state gave expression to the nation's character. Now it was five to ten, time to go to the funeral. And here I was at the cemetery. The coffin was carried slowly from the chapel to the graveside. At that moment motorcycles were revved up behind the cemetery wall, a helicopter appeared above the trees, intentionally drowning the cemetery, coffin, grave and souls of a thousand people with its Communist racket... God help me, I see that I have given way to hate, which as you will all testify has never happened before, and I take it back. Let me re-phrase it: a helicopter appeared, piloted by a slave to convey his master's message of contempt for the living and the dead.

"A fabric in six letters," said the older man.

"Calico," said the bright youth.

I started reading again:

"When Masaryk says: 'By violent or by peaceful means, using the plough or the sword? Peacefully, by means of the plough and our labour—that is the response of the Czech spirit and our history,' this would appear to be in keeping with the spirit of our development from the beginning of the nineteenth century up to the day of our independence. When the Mayor of Cork lay dying of hunger in a Dublin jail, an Irish crowd stood and knelt outside, singing religious songs."

Someone stepped up to the grave and started speaking, but not a word he spoke could be heard. One of the older mourners suggested that they sing the national anthem—but the roar of engines both on the ground and in the sky foiled their attempts to hit the right note.

"Those who favour pathos will be disappointed here," writes Peroutka. "When independence came on 28 October 1918, it was almost an idyllic occasion. And had it rained hard that day, it is possible we should be celebrating the 29th instead. The Communist movement, though stronger in our country than elsewhere, is moderate where action is concerned, and perhaps that is the reason for its comparatively large membership. And while our bourgeoisie might possibly incline towards fascism, it has absolutely no taste for such a semi-military existence."

"Nomad in four letters."

"Avar."

"When Bakunin, all bearded and black with gun powder, visited Bohemia, our rebel and satirist Havlíček found him objectionable and incomprehensible."

In the narrow spaces between the crosses, the mourners formed a line to throw flowers and spadefuls of earth onto the grave. Official photographers and cameramen were busy documenting the event, for good or ill.

Outside the window, a flurry of noise: doors banging, the sound of many people rushing about. It was a quarter to eleven. Someone knocked on the door. My companion left the room. When he returned, he said:

"So now it's all over. You can go home."

I ran to Národní Avenue, where I caught a taxi. Below the church of St Margaret I met the last stragglers returning from the funeral. At the cemetery gate I was merely asked for my identity card and photographed, but they let me in. I made my way across the silent, empty graveyard, passing among the tombstones and the crosses almost to the other end.

And there I did find a freshly dug grave. Which goes to show that you can't really miss a funeral. Only the living you can miss.

17 March 1977

On Heroism

I sometimes wonder if I'm mature enough to go to prison. It frightens me. We should all come to terms with this problem once we reach adulthood, and either behave in such a way as not to have to fear imprisonment or consider what is worth such a risk. It is hard to be locked up for something that will have ceased to excite anyone even before your sentence is up. That, I think, is what happened to the people who were imprisoned for the pre-election leaflets in 1972. And that is why I was greatly moved and encouraged by Jiří Müller's message from prison in which he advised people to act in an effective way and to avoid arrest.

It is one thing if they imprison someone who knows exactly what he is doing and why, and quite another when a young, immature person lands in jail, more or less by accident. I was amazed, for instance, by the fate of Karel Pecka (a leading dissident writer who made his literary debut in the sixties), who frittered his youth away in the uranium mines. For someone to be able to pick up the pieces of such a wrecked life and to give it a meaning and value I believe requires a kind of courage he surely did not possess before his prison experience. A normal human being, even a relatively calm one, if he opens a chess game badly, feels like sweeping the board clean and starting again. You can do that in a game of chess, but you can't do it in life.

Just to risk imprisonment is not in itself any kind of achievement, nor is it at all a good thing if during a dispute one side provokes the other to take a step which cannot be revoked without loss of honour, prestige, or authority. To do that can only make the situation worse. A man who suppresses the opinion of others is merely a censor; a censor, when resistance to censorship leads to imprisonment, becomes a dictator; the dictator who, in suppressing a protest demonstration, gives orders to fire at the crowd is a murderer. With the censor we could negotiate, and there was always a possibility that, as a result, his office would in time be abolished, and the censor himself would quietly accept some other desk job. In a murderer we have an enemy who cannot agree to any negotiation if he is not to end on the gallows.

However, where are the decent limits to such reflections?

No one can give a satisfactory reply to the question whether Charter 77 has made things better or worse, or how things would look today without it. Let us give up seeking such an answer, and let us add that the motives for our actions are only roughly parallel with political ones, the strongest impulses deriving from our character rather than our views. Charter 77 is today different from what it was in 1977. We have all had our share of trouble. I sometimes hear complaints that it is no longer as nice as it used to be. To this I would say that anyone who doesn't agree with what those who remain active and committed are doing, should withdraw quietly and undemonstratively and not hamper the work of those who are left. Each and every one of us can try and find methods which suit him best. If some team of people under threat decides to re-define its internal structure and tighten its rules, it can hardly expect to be understood by the public at large. While, on the one hand, a free man is put off by demands for absolute unity, on the other, the majority of sensible people tend to regard the increasingly heroic actions of an increasingly diminishing platoon of fighters as more and more their own personal affair. I mean this generally, as it applies to all shades of opinion.

Most people are well aware of their own limits and refrain from actions whose consequences they would be unable to bear. Anyone who, in a cool season, persuades people to take on more, should not be surprised when they break. An instinctive fear of hunger prevents a healthy and sensible person from feeling sympathy for someone who, in his own and the general cause, goes on hunger-strike. A matter of life and death? The sensible person gets cold feet and tries to find a way of dissociating himself from it at least a little. Psychologists and politicians cannot expect heroism in everyday life except when the whole environment is literally ionised by radiation from some powerful source. Heroic deeds are alien to everyday life. They are special events, which ought to be reported. They flourish in exceptional situations, but these must not be of long duration. A mass psychosis of heroism is a fine thing, provided there are in the vicinity some sober minds who have access to information and contacts and who know what's to be done afterwards.

I make a distinction between heroism and the integrity of the ordinary man. The ordinary man has a reserve of good habits and virtues, possesses his own integrity and knows how to protect it from erosion. Just as he doesn't like to see anyone acting in too dangerously defiant a manner, he also likes to reassure himself that quiet, honest toil is the best, even if it isn't particularly well rewarded, and that decent behaviour will find a decent response. Today, the main brunt of the attack is not directed so much at heroes as against what we used to consider the norm of work, behaviour and relationships. I would go so far as to say that the heroes are being given only measured doses of repression, which the regime feels duty-bound to administer. It is reluctant to do this because it doesn't want to give publicity to any heroes. The war should remain anonymous, without any recognisable faces or data. That is why the real explosive charges are scattered among the crowd, the intention being not to destroy anyone but rather to cause him to change his norms. A kind of neutron bomb: undamaged empty figures carry on walking to and from work.

We sometimes argue whether things are worse now than in the fifties, or if they are better. We can find sufficient evidence for both contentions. A truthful assessment will depend on how much we can gain from our present situation to benefit the future. The fifties had their revolutionary cruelty as well as their selfless enthusiasm. Certain sections of the population suffered grievously. Today there is no sign of any enthusiasm and, except in the case of a few excesses, no particular cruelty. Also, it no longer matters to which group anyone belongs. Violence has become humanised. The total surveillance of the entire population has been spread more gently over everyone and everything, it is devoid of the former spasms of hate. Is this better or worse? It is an attack on the very concept of normal life. I consider it more dangerous than in the fifties, yet we find it easier to live with.

Under the circumstances, every bit of honest work, every expression of incorruptibility, every gesture of goodwill, every deviation from cold routine, and every step or glance without a mask has the worth of a heroic deed. Our opponent, in particular, should find us ready—not to die for some rotten sacred cause—but to understand its positive aspects and to hold on to them. While heroism frightens people, giving them the truthful excuse that they are not made for it, everyone can bravely adhere to the norm of good behaviour at the price of acceptable sacrifice, and everyone knows it.

6 December 1978

(on the occasion of Karel Pecka's 50th birthday)

Jonas and the Monster

After Charter 77 came into being in January of that year, the secret police (STB) did their utmost to stamp out the budding human rights initiative. They harassed its signatories (Vaculík was one) at every step and called its spokesmen in for repeated interrogations. They also tried to persuade those involved to retract their signatures or to emigrate. When Ludvík Vaculík refused to do either, the Security's "dirty tricks" department tried to frame him on a charge of "distributing pornography". During a previous raid on his home, a certain Captain Martinovský had confiscated negatives of personal snapshots showing the writer cavorting in the nude in a cemetery. Some of these photos now appeared in the Prague popular weekly Ahoj, *which claimed that Vaculík had circulated them. Vaculík lodged a complaint, sued* Ahoj, *and accused the official news agency Ceteka of copying the photos. The final outcome was a draw—no charges were pressed against Vaculík, and, not surprisingly, the Interior Ministry was unable to trace the perpetrators.*

The rain was bucketing down in the streets of the city as I listened, in a gloomy office, to the recital of the results of the investigation. It was exactly as I had expected—and yet I was, nevertheless, in suspense.

It is now a quarter of a year since I received a summons to the Ministry of the Interior. The man I went to see was

about fifty-seven years old, quite tall and stocky, with a calm face and well-combed thinning hair, a lawyer by training and Jonas by name. He told me he had been instructed to investigate my complaint to the Prosecutor General of 26 January last. He gave me the obligatory official warning, the typist recorded the introductory formalities, and then he asked me:

"Are you in good health?"

"Why, yes, I think so," I replied, trying to formulate my answer as cautiously as possible, since everything was being taken down.

"Do you feel able to listen to the questions I'll put to you and to answer them with due care and consideration?"

"Yes, I believe so," I replied, thinking: I see. Patočka has died on them, and so they're taking out insurance.

"Should you by any chance feel tired, we can stop and give you a rest," said Mr Jonas. "Would you say that I or the other comrade present, or the comrade typist, are prejudiced against you?"

"Oh, no," I said, as amazed as no doubt the reader must be, and I gave expression to my amazement by asking: "What is this, a new type of interrogation?"

Mr Jonas, speaking in a superior tone and sounding really pleased with himself, explained: "That is the way we here at the Ministry Inspectorate do things because we consider it right to do so."

I was disappointed. Inspector Jonas—yes, let me call him an Inspector—took my letter from a file, handed it to me, and asked me if that was my letter. I nodded, but as he insisted I should examine it carefully, I took out my own copy and compared the two. Despite my permanent scepticism, I am always ready to acknowledge that things *may* take a turn for the better. I decided to accept Inspector Jonas at face value.

He said he was going to read out my letter, sentence by sentence, and would I comment as required. He ignored the first paragraph, in which I had written that the *Ahoj* weekly had printed an untrue report saying that I had circulated a series of pornographic photographs, because complaints against the press did not come under the jurisdiction of the Interior Ministry's Inspectorate. He dictated into the record my second paragraph, where I expressed the suspicion that the photographs were manufactured by the Czechoslovak News Agency, Ceteka.

"Have you any witnesses?" he asked.

"I should have thought that the activities of Ceteka are likewise outside your jurisdiction," I said.

It seemed that he accepted this, but on the other hand there was something to his objection:

"This investigation is being conducted at your request. You really must cooperate."

"First of all,"I said, "this investigation comes somewhat late in the day. The reason I wrote to the Prosecutor General was to warn him that a criminal offence was about to be committed. Had they acted quickly, they could have checked my story and prevented the offence taking place. It turned out that someone actually *did* manufacture those photographs and put them into circulation. Do you really think it could have been me?"

"To be frank with you," replied Inspector Jonas, "I

don't. But I have to ask you again, do you have any witnesses?''

"Yes, I do," I said, "but I'm not going to name them because they would suffer persecution if I did."

The Inspector looked round at his companions in astonishment and asked me why did I suppose so. I asked him whether he knew how those who had signed Charter 77 were being treated. He did not, and so I told him how people were dismissed from their jobs, had their driving licences taken away, their telephones disconnected, and how their lives were made difficult and miserable in all sorts of other ways. They all looked at me—Inspector Jonas, the other man, and the typist—as if they were hearing something quite incredible, and yet had no reason to think I was making it all up. I surrendered to my impression that I was talking to people who were working on so distant a site that they did not even know what their factory was producing, and I related a recent happening which I'm not going to record here. I'll save it up for another occasion when, once again, I'll have to respond to some dirty trick perpetrated by the boys in Bartolomějská (secret police headquarters). When I had finished, the Inspector laid his pencil on the desk and said:

"And did this really happen?"

"Yes, it did."

"All right, be that as it may, Mr Vaculík, you have made an accusation and now it's up to you to prove it. Did you know that Ceteka is also suing you?"

"Yes, I know that. If it comes to a court hearing where I have to defend myself, I'll produce my witnesses. But not before, as they'd only be silenced.''

Inspector Jonas called a halt to the proceedings and asked for coffee. However, I was not tired. I was wide awake with excitement, eager to make a correct assessment of the situation. I tend to judge what people might be capable of by the way they look. This chap and his taciturn colleague both looked decent, their faces weary from their non-combative office duties. They looked most unlikely ever to catch a criminal. Even though the Bartolomějská lot were subordinate to this Inspectorate, they invariably behaved as if they owned the whole of Prague. There you will come across policemen who themselves look like villains, and when someone like officer Martinovský is called to the Inspectorate to answer questions, the likes of Jonas must be well pleased to see the back of him. As we drank our coffee I said:

''I wonder, Mr Jonas, if all this is just intended to get me to give you the witnesses' names.''

''To be honest with you,'' he said, ''I don't believe you *have* any witnesses. I think you're just… shooting from the hip.'' And he acted out his words, like a left-handed gunfighter.

The interval over, the investigation continued with Inspector Jonas saying:

''I don't expect you to believe this, but I haven't been able to unearth a single one of these photographs.''

''They've hidden them well,'' I said, smiling. ''And yet, all the editorial offices boasted of having them!''

He shrugged—and I believed him. It was, in fact, only now, when I believed this piece of nonsense, that the strange investigation began to make sense to me.

There seemed to be three possibilities. One, somebody at the top had become confused as to what actually happened and wanted to find out. The scandal was beginning to smell, so they dispatched old Jonas to inspect the premises in question and report on how much was seeping out. Two, perhaps it was par for the course for such an unpopular institution, so vulnerable to any change in the political climate, to record its wrongdoing so as to be able to cleanse itself when trouble threatened. Perhaps they employed quite a few decent people here just for this purpose, as fall guys. And three, it was possible that they simply wanted those witnesses.

I tipped these nice people off as to where they were sure to find a batch of the photographs: in Bartolomějská Street. One of their teams had confiscated the pictures during the house search at the home of Věra Jirousová, they had entered it in the record. I asked Inspector Jonas how he intended to go about his investigation. He said he'd have the usual laboratory tests carried out, obtain some expert testimony and interrogate some people.

As I write these lines, my eyes rest on a stone cannon ball lying on one of my shelves, and it is with difficulty that I overcome a feeling of distaste for this Republic and carry on typing.

"You won't discover anything, you know. And should you look like doing so, they'll sack you."

He smiled. Out of the corner of my eye I saw a hint of a smile also on the taciturn face to the side of me. The typist's lips twitched as well.

"You really are a sceptic, aren't you," said Inspector

Jonas. "Did you not expect us to treat you as we have done?"

I confessed. I could not imagine that those who ordered something rotten to be done would now allow someone to be punished for it. I would be quite content if at least they issued internal instructions forbidding such conduct in future. This, surely, cannot be the way a State organ behaves. With such thoughts in my mind I had, in September 1976, written a letter to the Minister of the Interior. The letter never reached him, and the copy which I had was confiscated by Martinovský.

"If you were so distrustful, why did you decide to write to the Prosecutor General, and why did you have your letter published abroad?"

"I felt I was in a tight spot. I wanted to make things more difficult for the perpetrators. And by publishing the letter I wanted to get the Prosecutor General to react. Perhaps I owe him an apology for the tone of my letter. But those who took it on themselves to attack me this way shouldn't be allowed to get away with it, at least where I'm concerned. And so, even though it makes life difficult for me and my family, I'll do my best to show that a naked STB is repugnant."

Inspector Jonas's features grew a little harder, the typist's fingers froze above her machine. Then Jonas read a paragraph in which I complained of extortion and described the house search at my place in April 1975.

"You signed the protocol confirming the number of confiscated negatives," said Jonas.

"That I doubt. And last January they even confiscated

that protocol."

He dropped his pencil and asked: "They did what?"

"Yes, they took my copy of the protocol. Intending to produce a forgery. Do you think they can do that?"

He got up, fetched some papers and read from them: "Item seventy-two, two envelopes for negatives..."

"*Were* there any negatives in them?" I asked. "And if so, what of?"

"There seems to be something wrong here...," he said, shaking his head.

I took out my copy of the protocol the police made after this year's house search and read item thirty-four: "Eleven files of correspondence. What correspondence? What about?"

"Yes, I noticed that," said Inspector Jonas.

I don't feel like narrating the rest of the discussion—it's too boring. Let us therefore cut to me and Inspector Jonas going down in the elevator, with Inspector Jonas uttering these wonderful words:

"To be telling the truth is one thing, Mr Vaculík, to prove it quite another."

A bright May sun was shining outside. The best of luck, my good man!

Some three weeks later I had a visit from Colonel Noga, who brought back my negatives, all carefully counted and recorded. One day I'll look at them and find out what is in those pictures.

And yesterday I called in for the result. It was raining cats and dogs, and I felt damp in spite of my umbrella. Maybe that is why I was less alert than usual and can offer the reader few nuggets from this particular excursion. Inspector Jonas received me on his own, sat me down, and handed me his decision. The document said that my complaint to the Prosecutor General had been

d e f e r r e d

"as our investigation did not produce any evidence that any criminal offence or misdemeanor had been committed in the matter complained of". I had, it was stated, not been able to establish "anything substantive which would have led to the clarification of the circumstances mentioned by the complainant". Neither did the interrogation of certain individuals, or the expert testimony of a handwriting expert, a biologist and others provide any proof of a criminal offence or misdemeanor by members of the STB. It had likewise proved impossible to ascertain who had duplicated the pornographic material, and where this was done. None of the objects investigated was of Czechoslovak origin or manufacture.

—Signed, Major Lumír JONAS.

In my wet and uncomfortable state I could not think of a wittier response than to say: "Oh, and what...how...yes, very good."

Inspector Jonas helpfully pointed to a huge, thick file in front of him. "I interrogated a number of people. Including Matura—you know him as Martinovský. I even, thanks to you, managed to get hold of the photographs."

"What did you find out?"

He leafed through the file, then read: "An orange-coloured envelope made of glazed paper 0.2mm thick, of untraceable origin."

"Anything else?" I asked.

"Yes. We found that the stamps had been affixed by licking. I can even tell you the sender's blood group: AI."

I was astonished. God, why did they stop there? They had almost got him!

Inspector Jonas asked me to confirm with my signature that I had been given the document he had drafted, and he informed me that I was entitled to appeal against the decision within three days.

"I shan't appeal," I said.

"As you wish. But it is your right to do so," he added in the tone they at the Interior Ministry Inspectorate consider correct.

It was still pouring beautifully outside. As I put distance between myself and the Inspector, I felt that I had won a kind of victory, but I could not say exactly what it was. As if I had been told that I was definitely in the right and that I could now try and find my man myself, with the help of his blood group, I gaze at that wonderfully simple instrument lying on the shelf. From a literary point of view that would be the ideal way to finish the story—but on the other hand, from a literary point of view, this is enough. Let's consider it done.

And in real life? In real life both I and my readers know that all we have to do is wait. They will kill each other off themselves because that is what they are like.

23 August 1977

(copy to Major Jonas)

The Spring Is Here

I spent the night before the first day of spring in an Indian hammock called *amaka*, which comes from Nicaragua. The following day there was a coup in neighbouring Guatemala. These constant coups must be absolutely dreadful. On the other hand, it is also dreadful when there isn't even a glimmer of change for a long time. I don't really know which is worse. The hammock was surprisingly comfortable to sleep in. If it's more than six yards long and well slung, you don't wake up with an aching back and you get up next morning feeling refreshed, as if you'd been taken down after an airing; the air does not leave you feeling squashed, does not crease your tummy or squeeze your joints. The Indians sleep in the nude, a whole family to a hammock, or so I was told, and they multiply most pleasantly in it. In the morning, my host did not even ask me what I had dreamed about. And, as luck would have it, I had not dreamed anything, not even privately.

Last March, our old teacher, Mrs Svatoňová, reached her ninetieth year. We therefore drove to Brumov for a little celebration. The first thing she asked me was, what did those two Russian spaceships find on Venus. As Mrs

Svatoňová's eyesight isn't what it used to be, I described the landscape up there as best I could: reddish rocks and dust, temperature of four hundred degrees or more, and pressure of ninety non-atmospheres caused by unbreathable gases. Said Mrs Svatoňová: "Oh dear, and is it worth it?"

"Oh, yes," I replied, but Madla was quick to correct me: "Of course it isn't, Mrs Svatoňová. It's one-upsmanship, that's all. Now the Americans are going up in their shuttle."

Now, the old lady is quite capable of figuring out the ideological aspect of space research for herself, but she does need a little help with the technical side. I therefore expostulated on the novel feature of the Columbia aircraft which can return to earth and be used again.

"Well now, that really is clever," she said, "Perhaps mankind will one of these days come to work together on something sensible. And what about our gold? People here, you know, expected that when the Americans returned it to us, we would all feel the benefit somehow and find more in the shops, but that's all nonsense, isn't it."

"What do you think, Mrs Svatoňová," cried Madla, "I wouldn't be surprised if that gold never even arrived."

"It arrived all right," I assured them. "They drove with it along Příkopy right through the centre of Prague."

But of course, who knows *what* they were carrying, I said to myself as I strode along the crest of the railway tunnel through which a goods train was rumbling. The mud had lost its top layer of frost and I had to step carefully. There was snow in the furrows. Looking round about me I discovered that where there used to be a labyrinth of stony paths, only one now remained, the others having been ploughed up and turned into a field which was flecked with the green of the winter crop. Up above the vast expanse a crow was cawing. I had had no intention of coming this way, indeed had explicitly forbidden myself to do so, but my legs carried me willy-nilly. I followed my behaviour with sarcastic detachment, determined to be very sceptical. It was therefore with a considerable amount of scepticism that I viewed the mighty barrier of oaks and lindens, pacing out the distance between the taboo tree and the disused well which, as far as I was concerned, I could open up any time. Peering out through the veil of leaves I looked from afar into one of the square pits which had been dug there and, shrugging my shoulders ironically, I realised how it would all end: everything here would be felled, burned or allowed to rot, while new undergrowth was sprouting up everywhere as the rising sun gleamed on the dew.

I returned by way of the cemetery, where I stood a while by my parents' grave and also by the as yet unoccupied plot no 55, from where I shall have a good view of the church, brewery, and high school.

In the afternoon Miroslav Zikmund came to congratulate the old teacher. The first thing she wanted to know was: "And which would you say is the most decent state in the world?"

The experienced traveller thought about this and then started telling her about Nepal, where there lived very poor but very dignified and gentle people...

"But you see," I interrupted him, "Mrs Svatoňová meant it in a political sense. In which country does the state treat its citizens most decently? And she expected you to say England.''

The traveller thought again, but Mrs Svatoňová put in: "No, I wasn't thinking of England, really. Perhaps in earlier times, but today, I would have expected you to suggest Scandinavia.''

The traveller sighed and told her he didn't know Europe because he and his friend Hanzelka, with whom he had done all his travelling twenty, thirty years ago and wrote all those books, had left Europe until last, when they would be more tired—or lazy—and now of course they aren't allowed to travel anywhere.

I felt a surge of hatred. Mrs Svatoňová said in her husky voice: "You have seen a lot of the world, haven't you, my boy. Where does all this hatred and violence come from? Does it spring up of its own accord, or is it all organised by somebody who profits by it?''

I have censored the traveller's thoughtful reply. After all, we're not in Scandinavia.

Returning to Prague, we saw fresh snow in the mountains. And back home I learned that they had released Karel Kyncl, Ruml junior, Eva Kanturková and Jiřina Šiklová from custody. But one swallow does not a summer make.

March 1982

How to Survive 1984

The courage with which we have entered the year 1984 will one day amaze future generations. From all sides we are bombarded by evil presentiments, ominous horoscopes, bad news from the fronts, failed Soviet peace initiatives—what lies in store? And on top of all that, last year's potato crop was half rotten. The world seems to stand in awe of Orwell's date and hardly anyone believes in the prophecy of Amalrik's. I too, feel as if an unbearable weight rested on my shoulders, and I'm hard put to it to imagine that we shall continue leading normal lives, that is, according to our intelligence and capabilities.

A special landmark for those of us in Czechoslovakia who do not go in for terrorism has to be the pre-Christmas bomb allegedly discovered in the Kotva department store. When I tried to figure out whose criminal might have been responsible, it occurred to me that the police, who are bound to come and search my home too, looking for explosives, will again, as if shell-shocked, confiscate my manuscripts, books, letters and photographs. And so I sit here among my depleted shelves, prepared to face the future better than I should have expected, with just one "incriminating" sheet

of paper in the typewriter (the one you are reading) which, should the doorbell ring, I'd have to rip out of the machine, tear up and flush doen the toilet because, as yet, I have not reached the point where I'd admit to myself that I no longer wish to write, as I was saying last December. I said that because I found that my writing was having a highly depressing effect on me, so how much worse will it be this year? Let me go on record then that I can see no other way of dealing with this ominous year except to ignore it, and I hope this bit of advice will help my readers to survive 1984 as best they can, for next year is supposed to be better, if we live that long.

There is one item left over from last year that I have to deal with, and that is the New Year's Eve flight of a Prague family who escaped to Yugoslavia, via Austria.

The man (31) is an actor whom I have seen both on stage (in the experimental theatre) and in small parts on TV. His is a personality that could never settle for conventional casting in which he would grow old reciting the words of the classics or of dramatists sanctioned by the state. He needs his own personal theatre, or at least his own main part. For that, there is insufficient space in this country, and perhaps too many actors. The woman (29) is a writer. I have read a children's book by her that was published here, two of her plays, one of which was about to be staged in Prague but was then banned and allowed to be performed only in the provinces, and a short story. They refused to publish her second book and wanted to prevent her getting it published abroad. Recently, they stopped her from going on a short study trip, giving as their excuse that she was registered as a cleaner, which is what she was, using her talent for writing in her spare time, whereas they no doubt realise that *they* have no such extra talent. But all this is part and parcel of conditions here today, conditions that serve to wear down every independent-minded person, including born cleaners, and it is understandable that some might want to escape from it all.

It is also true that an actor, just like a singer or athlete, feels that he has only a limited time in which to make his mark. And a writer needs to be able to publish if he or she is to keep on writing; his time span is a longer one, but the obstacles placed in his path by our unconquerable, evil powers-that-be shorten that span as well as his life. Well, there it is, that's how things are here today, our contemporary form of the old tuberculosis which killed off many better talents before us, our modern counter-reformation with its banned books and persecuted writers.

Those two young people, when they were given a friendly reception on the other side, said—I don't know exactly what words they used—that they wanted to preserve their future work.—1. Does this mean that the Czech writer intends, with the aid of a translator, to write several good German books, but with Czech accents on the names of her characters?—2. Maybe, however, she wants to carry on fighting against the evil she has escaped from, in which case, however, she has quit the scene of the action.—3. It is, of course, possible for an artist to take his subject-matter to a calmer venue and write it up in some non-seasonal fashion, and in that case let's wish her many years in which to do it. But the world is full of various kinds of evil, and it has its own fighters doing their best to combat it. So that they will hardly notice the arrival of another, while here he or she will be sadly missed.

I would not be writing this if these two people were presenting their largely personal case in terms of their earlier suffering. But the actor was allowed to act. And the writer left at a time when one of our theatres was putting on another of her plays—they had already booked a hotel room for her and had refreshments and a bouquet laid on, everything except an apology from her for her absence. True, she did speak on a foreign (or, as it is officially called hostile) radio program, thanking the theatre director for his courage and the actors for the way they had managed to understand all the nuances of her text. (Here in Prague we don't even dare praise Johanides or Sloboda in Bratislava, in case our praise leads to their banning.) And yet, what else was she to do? How to underline her persecution and the courage needed to stage her plays?

They also said, I understand, that they wished to save their children. I have met them: a girl of nine and a boy of five...two such normal, ordinary kids that it makes you wonder why, of all the children in Prague, they should be saved from burning.

An instinctive escape from the expected epicentre. Running away from the burden of one's destiny. It lacks that overblown socialist collective responsibility for the fate of the world, but also the Christian humility which makes one bear whatever cross it is one's lot to carry.

But not all the paths leading from our human crossroads have been trodden yet.

January 1984

Fences

When you come to think of it, the world is in the hands
of inferior people. All kinds of incompetents and roughnecks
appoint all kinds of watchdogs to keep us in line; thieves
and murderers have provided us with a corps of police and
detectives; power-hungry fellows who, if they needed our
confidence to do so, wouldn't be able to stay in office,
burden us with secret policemen, narks and directors. And
so we, who never so much as commit a litter offence, are
not even permitted to put up a tent at the end of a day's
outing. We have never so much as stolen a candle, yet we
find all the churches locked against us. Not in our wildest
dreams would we invade the territory of another nation or
have designs on their property, nevertheless we are forced
to undergo long years of suffering in the army; and while
we of course also don't wish to be dominated or robbed
by evil neighbours, we are not allowed to keep our arms
at home.

Everywhere, they put up fences against us: fences of iron,
wood, words. There is less and less room for free movement
and free action. They tell us that this is due to the population growth. Really! What has happened is that people's

sense of responsibility without coercion has been enfeebled, the upbringing of those charged with bringing up the young ruined, the nation's conscience dulled. That is why we can no longer rely on such instruments of self-administration as we used to have in public opinion, established custom, a sense of shame or a reluctance to sin. All this also mars the character of fences: intended to protect what is inside against wrongdoers, too often they conceal the wrongdoing that is going on inside.

I heard tell about an old quarry next to a lake, and I went there to have a look. NO ENTRY said a sign someone had put up on the field path. No signature. Who prohibits entry, and by what right? I decided to ignore it. If the sign had carried the signature of the management of the quarry, I would have known that they were still in operation. If there had been the signature of the local health authority, it would have told me that they wished to save me from possible injury. The quarry formed several terraced layers with a gorgeous lake at the bottom. On the other side I could see some tents and a flag at the top of a pole. Several people standing on the lowest level of the rock were watching two frogmen splashing about in the water around a coloured buoy. I realised that divers were undergoing training here today. Never mind, I thought, I'll come another time. But my conciliatory mood was shattered by that mocking sign: See? By way of exception, and if organised, everything is allowed.

One day I wanted to have lunch at the Black Horse in Vodička Street. There were plenty of free tables, but in the door they had a notice: Please wait here—the headwaiter will seat you. When he turned up, he pointed to three men who were just coming down the stairs behind me, and said: "I'll put you with these three gentlemen." That made me really mad. "No," I said, "I'll sit on my own at that little table for two." And I went in. You see, I explained (in my mind, guiltily) to the waiter, I have no wish to listen to what those three gentlemen are talking about, I'd rather be left alone with my own thoughts.

At last, I'm told, they have closed the mountain paths in the Tatras. People are now allowed there for only two months in the year, and then it seems only if accompanied by a guide. Conservationists consider it a victory, but in fact it has finally put paid to our communing with the mountains. It all began when they built hotels, asphalt roads and cable railways for the privileged, and it ends with us being allowed to go to the mountains in order to sit in hotels. Mountains should be free of access all the year round, especially when the weather turns frosty and the rain and snow come, all the way up from the foothills for people to ramble, to pitch a tent and, where conditions allow, light a fire.

Rožnov in the Beskydy Mountains is a place where they manufacture TV sets. They are now to introduce a production line for colour screens, and this will pollute the Bečva River. Medical experts, nature lovers, and even the local National Committee have lodged protests with the government. Which, to no one's surprise, has come to the following decision: the lucrative manufacture of colour TVs is to start straightaway, the non-lucrative measures to save the river from pollution will be "put in the plan".

What misfortune to have organisations and institutions to protect health, nature and historical relics instead of having people everywhere who, before they make a decision, take all these things into account. As it is, it's always those whose thinking is warped by commercial and profit motives, by a slavish adherence to trends and fashions, by instincts of self-preservation and fears of loss of face or of sinecure who come out on top. Such individuals may even pass decent laws, but then play fast and loose with them wherever they can. Just take a peep into the greenery of one of those so-called protected country regions or national parks: like so many snails in the grass you'll find a multitude of officials organising the devastation all around.

I took some friends to see Brumov Castle. Emerging round the bend behind the brewery, I stopped in my tracks: an iron fence had been erected all along the ponds. I could not believe my eyes. There had always been a sign here, prohibiting access to the banks of the ponds. Everyone knew that the water was used by the brewery to make beer, and while people did climb up on to the bank, they respected the spirit of the prohibition: no one peed in the water, no one bathed in the ponds or let their cows do so. It used to be one of the town's favourite spots where people went for a Sunday stroll. I learned that originally the intention was to put up an even taller fence, with spikes turned outwards and barbed wire on top, but the local committee had at least managed to talk the authorities out of that and achieve a compromise. And why a fence at all? So that people shouldn't throw dead animals in the water or tractor drivers wash their machines there. And so those inferior

people, of whom there are perhaps three here—or thirty?—
have just set up yet another fence for three thousand.

If only I were lord of the manor at Brumov, I'd go for
a cheaper and more just solution. I'd have these people
brought to the castle and given twenty-five of the best. Out-
moded, you say? All right, then, I'd open a kind of research
institute there, to which this kind of people would be
brought from the entire Brumov region and I'd carry out
a scientific experiment to discover how many blows with
a stick it takes to cure them.

June 1984

Thus Spake Švejk

Jaroslav Hašek and Franz Kafka were born 100 years ago.

Švejk is one of those characters who is still very much with us here in Prague.

When I was at the appropriate age of about twenty, I too read *The Good Soldier Švejk*, and I laughed a lot. I knew nothing then of the world fame attached to this piece of literature, nor did it occur to me to look for any particular "message" in it. As far as I was concerned, it was the story of an ordinary bloke who, while somewhat dumb, nevertheless realised that if only he handled his stupidity adroitly, it would bring him certain advantages which he could then not-so-innocently put to good use. Ever since the book first appeared, literary experts have argued about the proportions of stupidity and cunning doled out by Jaroslav Hašek when he created this famous character, but all their learned researches cannot improve on the simple question posed by First Lieutenant Lukáš when first confronted by his new batman: "Listen, Švejk, are you really such a simpleton?"

It came as a great surprise to me when, in later years, I learned of the existence of what I might call Švejkology, and I'm invariably offended when foreigners try to explain Švejk by reference to the Czech national character, or worse still, the Czech national character by reference to Švejk. And, dear friends, you really blew it, you gave the game away when you tried to complete the account of Švejk's adventures by way of your Brecht! Švejk's story simply can't be completed—he exists like an ornament on the façade of Old Europe, and this has long ago been placed in an open-air museum, where we go to gaze at Švejk's endearing idiocy.

Since the First World War, three generations—here and the world over—have been delighted by Švejk's antics. In civvies, this man made the rounds of Prague pubs, doing odd jobs and buying and selling dogs. In the army, he carried out only the simplest of orders, doing his damndest to eat and drink and keep his nose clean so as to avoid anything resembling trouble or unpleasantness. Like the plague he avoided brutality, of which he himself was quite incapable. This defencelessness of his of course makes us like him, but let's be honest: he was a primitive soul, and no way would we contemplate living in close proximity with him.

And so we go on smiling condescendingly at this character, and it never occurs to any of us to wonder what would happen if this "simpleton" were to disappear for a while and then return with the rank of First Lieutenant. Now *there's* an idea how to complete the story of the good soldier Švejk, don't you think?

In our country, an incredible amount of time and effort has been devoted to this crazy experiment...I have for many years now been a "regular"—though without the customary pleasure—in one Prague establishment of ill-repute, which I visit involuntarily, to sit in the unfriendly company of men in front of whom I feel as if I were confronted by the very countenance that Josef Lada, Švejk's illustrator and co-founder, established as the symbol of a certain somatic type. A face not furrowed by a single risky thought, eyes in whose depths you will never discern the slightest humorous or understanding gleam. I keep my cool, even though I would be quite entitled to yell, maintain a poker face when desperately tempted to burst out laughing, and keep saying "I don't know" when I could just as easily and with impunity say "I know".

"Okay, Mr Vaculík, why don't you tell us…" says the fellow, who, since the First World War, has learned perfectly to match the colour of his shirt and tie with that of his jacket and to use after-shave; while I, in order to gain a precious second, quickly anticipate his unfinished questions, which are really in the nature of fishing expeditions: What do I do all day, since I don't have a job? What do I live on, since I don't get anything published? What contacts do I have with émigrés? How do I manage to send my manuscripts abroad?

"What do you know about the Dictionary of Czechoslovak Writers, which is being published by an émigré publishing house in Toronto?"

"That's a scientific study," I reply, thoroughly prepared, "containing names and facts that might otherwise be forgotten or erased, but as this has no connection with any criminal act, I refuse to talk about it."

"Oh, come on, that's what you always say—but if there's no criminal act involved, why do you refuse to testify?"

the man goes on, applying logic as round as a shaven skull.

For the umpteenth time I try to explain why I don't consider him entitled to have that question answered. Would it ever have been conceivable, in Švejk's day in old Bohemia, for police or firemen to pose as literary experts? While Hašek's Švejk is the embodiment of biological idiocy, *our* Švejk represents institutionalised incompetence, ignorance armed with full powers. You would think that teachers would teach their pupils how to read, parents instil good manners, and that anyone who in his youth had indulged in at least a little thought would one day be bound to reach a frontier beyond which he perceives an unattainable spiritual world. This frontier is different for each one of us—after all, human wisdom is not measured by how far we have managed to push it or penetrate beyond it but, on the contrary, by the respect we show for the unattainable, the mysterious, or simply the *different*. This has nothing at all to do with the kind of education one has had, but rather depends on how much thought, feeling, and perhaps suffering has gone into one's perception of one's own place in life.

In the case of these people, this just doesn't work. The man confronting me was no congenital idiot, but he had veered off the natural human path and accepted a role in which he could not help seeming and acting like one. And when we come into contact with such people it is always difficult to differentiate between their two main characteristics; that is, their human nature and their anti-human (or rather, non-human) calling. They act and express themselves as if they were not part of mankind's long evolution, as if nothing was owed to the past, as if they and they alone were here to legislate and preserve. In physics, matter is opposed by anti-matter; here we are dealing with anti-thought.

The men facing me across the desk don't know, for instance, how I have come to the conclusion that the individual is more than the state, that the state is nothing but an artificial and changeable human invention, and that's why people are constantly attempting to reform it. Once I told one of them: "The degree of civil liberty is not measured by the way the state treats millions of those who agree with it, but rather how it treats, let us say, a dozen who don't." He just looked at me, and said nothing. I wasn't at all sure he had understood me, and so I went on: "You know what I mean, where there is agreement, freedom doesn't come into it—freedom only begins where dissent begins. But that is just where *you* come in with your repression." He didn't understand. This chap probably does not, even at home after work, nor at night before he falls asleep, reflect on what new things he has heard that day, as used to be the case in Bohemia. Because the next time he was exactly the same.

"You aren't a member of the Writers' Union, nor are you registered with the Literary Fund," he said to me on one occasion, "so that means you're no writer."

Oh dear, I thought, who *is* a writer, anyway—but when you're dealing with someone who obviously believes that writers are bred like calves in state cowsheds, or like policemen in those institutions of theirs, you have to speak simply and to the point. "Hašek also wasn't a member of the Writers' Union,'' I told him. "Oh, but Hašek wrote against Austria-Hungary,'' replied Švejk. "whereas you write with double meanings and between the lines.'' This made me angry, and so I decided to burden him with the following rejoinder: "The more ways a literary work can be interpreted, the more interesting it is, the wider its meaning, the longer it is likely to survive.'' He thought about this, then reached for the ashtray and tapped the ash off his cigarette. "We shall definitely not permit anyone,'' he said, using the simplest of terms, as if he had abandoned all hope of explaining his anti-world to me, "to sully the good name of the Republic.''

Thus spake Švejk, who in this land of ours has contaminated the air, water, people, work, meat, the very clay with which bricks are made (I'm sitting by the window through which I can see the roof opposite, repaired only a few years ago, which has again lost a great many tiles, now lying in the gutter), and just about everything.

When the stove in Hašek's Švejk's room started to give off smoke, he asked Mrs Müller to clean it. In fundamental everyday matters that simpleton behaved quite sensibly. But our Švejk, the one whose story has been brought up to date, is not like that: when the forests in the centre of the country begin to die because the powers-that-be have polluted the air, he will calculate how much timber they will yield and how much that will fetch in Austria, and then, instead of firs, he will order birches to be planted. When a part of the country is declared a protected area, a nature reserve or park, luck will have it that some idiot will discover coal there, so that just when preservation should start, Švejk will give orders for the construction of a coalmine. When, as a result of our deteriorating environment destroyed by toxic emissions and radiation, the country suffered an outbreak of disease and genetic changes, Švejk forbade all this to be reported, and immediately felt healthier.

The involuntary interview is over and I'm allowed to leave. As I am about to open the door he stops me with yet one more question: "When did you last see your friends in Bratislava?" Deliberately I reply: "Two years ago." He smiles, knowing it was last month. He knows because he has my phone tapped. "Oh, right, goodbye then," he says jovially, extending his right hand. "And why don't you write something nice for us for a change? Time flies, how much more can you get done?" How friendly of him, you might be tempted to think. But this Švejk of the Orwell era merely wants to let me know that *he* knows I've been suffering from writer's block for weeks now, staring at a blank sheet of paper in my typewriter.

Once I told him that literature was, in a sense (in its truest sense), superior to governments and could not therefore be ruled by their opinions, moods and tantrums. History, after all, shows that nothing lasts forever—just think back to the patriotic writers at the time of the Austro-Hungarian Empire, for instance. He pondered this for a second, and then said: "That's possible. So that you're really just unlucky, Mr Vaculík."

But I understand: let those who invented Švejk put up with him.

November 1984

My Table at the Belvedere

The frost in Prague 7 has eased up at last. It is early afternoon, and the day is light grey. The almost empty coffee-
house is half taken up with "Reserved" notices. In the two
hours I have been here, not one person turned up at the
reserved tables. The waiters are thus simply herding the
patrons into one corner so as to save themselves the trouble of running all over the place.

As far as I'm concerned, I like to pick my own table
according to the view it affords, the lighting, my mood,
or according to what I am going to be discussing, and with
whom. Someone had just left my table and the café per-
sonnel had not yet had time to substitute a "Reserved"
notice for the empty coffee cup. And so I am sitting, all
on my own, in the western wing of the coffee-house on the
first floor of the Belvedere Hotel, by the window, looking
out at Belcredi Avenue. The room is L shape, its southern
arm affording a view of a side street with the Ponrepo
cinema, which I have never visited, and the Security
building, in which I was a regular guest for a number of
years. The corner of the room is rounded, the tables standing on a raised podium. I suppose a band used to sit and

play there once upon a time.

It is said that in every café, wine cellar or restaurant there are certain tables that are bugged. That's quite possible, but it is hardly something that need worry the general public: who could be interested in that kind of gossip? Bugging is usually aimed at selected people and carried out at certain times. Here at the Belvedere I would guess it is in that rounded corner, but not installed in the tables but in the railing below the podium—that is where, some years ago, Major P. was waiting for me, the author meeting his avid reader. I came fifteen minutes early on purpose, and yet he was already there. Now I give those tables a miss. And it is why the other day, when an American journalist met me to ask if I could arrange a meeting with the poet Jaroslav Seifert, we sat where I'm sitting today.

Who knows where I sat in 1970 with the man who had come to request that I write an appeal urging railwaymen to strike, saying he would distribute it in North Bohemia. Nothing came of this, since I couldn't summon up any enthusiasm for the project; after all, I don't even take the train to North Bohemia.

I cannot remember when I came here for the first time, with whom, or what for—I don't often visit the Belvedere, only when something important is up. I never used to be in the habit of haunting cafés, but now it is different: this year I'm going to frequent them in order to write. I was always amused by stories of poets, journalists and conmen going to the coffee-houses to "work" in the olden days of Austria-Hungary: they would sit there reading all the Imperial and European papers, drinking wine and smoking their cigars in true lordly fashion.

My table is the last but one in the row by the windows. Every time I come here I deliberate which way I should sit—facing "her" or with my back to her? So that she shouldn't distract me just today when I, too, am starting to "work" here, I turn my back on her: the statue of a nude woman in a niche in the wall. Long ago I inspected her from head to toe: a mockingly sensuous expression, fine bosom, jutting left hip...and a man's severed head on a platter. "Coffee and tonic water, please."

I prepare a sheet of paper, wanting to write. But what am I to write about? Of course, describe what I can see from my vantage point. So, here goes: looking out of the window I see people picking their way through the salted slush. I can see the aforementioned side street and the Security building. There I used to sit far more often than here, facing my unwanted reader, who when we met at the café always offered me a chair that was pushed some way from the table or strangely positioned, perhaps to negate the impression that we were sitting in a coffee-house. But of course it could have been for the purposes of bugging our conversation or, it occurred to me, radiation. But since I don't incline to paranoia I invariably dismissed the idea and let them irradiate me.

In front of me I see the interior of the café with some five patrons. On the right, by the wall, four men in semi-military dress are sitting together. Behind them a solitary young woman in a heavy rollneck sweater and with a fur hat on her head, sitting alone facing the door. Whom is she waiting for? I do not like the tables by the wall, preferring those by the window. Year before last a stranger—a Czech who was working for an international organisation—offered to deliver whatever I gave him on his trips abroad. It was right here at this very table—coincidence?—I let him take the chair facing the statue and watched his face as we talked, then turned down his offer.

Four elderly ladies, about seventy I should think, came in, somewhat agitated. There was nobody to take their coats in the cloakroom, and they could not decide where to sit or where to deposit all their apparel. And that young woman is no longer alone, she is greeting an old, dried-up, greyhaired man, who is obviously apologising to her. He takes off his overcoat and then they notice the group of men at the next table and they immediately move away, the young woman carrying her glass of lemon tea, going over to the raised podium in the corner...I look on in suspense...they mount the podium, that's good. They sit down at a table at which a pregnant friend once asked me what we were to do. That table affords a very good view: if the hotel were to start moving down Belcredi Avenue, that would be the place for the driver.

Another thing that used to impress me about those tales of olden times was how in the days when the coffee-houses offered their customers various European newspapers to read, they knew how—with the aid of the coachmen, messengers, cloakroom ladies, waiters or managers—to conduct various love affairs, intrigues, adventures. I wonder with whose help I might be able to do something important. Something that brooks no delay does occur to me, and I go to the phone and call Zdeněk. Day after tomorrow he is due to leave for a cure in the spa of Konstantinovy Lázně. He reacts joyously: "I've been trying to get hold of you...where *are* you?...Okay, wait for me, I'll come over."

Fifteen minutes later he comes in and looks around the almost empty room. I rise to my feet, he sees me and, beaming like the sun itself, crosses over to where I am sitting. I place him opposite me, he gazes over my head and begins to laugh, discreetly, in a whisper: "I see...so this, you say, is your favourite spot?" A waiter comes up, and Zdeněk orders: "Well, I'd like...ehm...also a coffee. And...what else?" When the waiter departs, Zdeněk gets down to brass tacks: "You know I'm leaving day after tomorrow...and, well, you mustn't be annoyed, I just didn't have time..."

"Better leave this for later, Zdeněk," I interrupt him, pointing with my thumb in the direction of the naked lady. He takes a closer look, is about to say something, but then the waiter reappears with his coffee. When he is gone, Zdeněk makes sure he has left and tears open the paper sachet containing sugar. He pours half of it into his cup, stirs the coffee, stares reflectively over my head and says: "Isn't it terrible...the fate of men."

January 1985

Walking down Příkopy

On the threshold of The Savarin I stopped short: should I really venture into that smoke-filled atmosphere? But duty called, and a reminiscence of the summer of 1979 drew me inside; sitting down in a cubicle by the window I ordered a Viennese coffee. I had to have somewhere to sit and consider a few more questions for the government. In the meantime, the elderly ladies at the next table will, using two different sets of spectacles, show each other some old photographs. Everything here is elderly and worn-out, almost due for the scrap-heap. Though, of course, things could be cleaned, repaired and renovated, but no doubt instead it will all get discarded and new things bought in its place—that's the way the economy is run in our country. I'll have to have a word with the minister responsible when the occasion arises.

What this government of ours is afraid of, and why—that's easy enough to answer, though unnecessary. But why does it not conduct itself so that it does not *have* to be afraid, that's more difficult, and I would not want to attempt an answer without consulting the government first. That's all very well, but how do I manage it? Which one of us is likely to get invited out somewhere, and there "I happened to bump into the Prime Minister, and so mentioned it to him"? Or, to put it more accurately, which member of the government is likely to have the good fortune to meet one of *us?* Our paths have diverged so completely that even our impressions from our travels are now mutually incommunicable.

What a sad thing it must be to rule this country these days: whom can these people fully trust, on whom can they rely? Whenever I see them, those shadowy figures on my TV screen, as they cheerlessly climb into airplanes, I can feel their isolation—they have no one but themselves. When one of them goes abroad, the others, no matter how much work they might have back at the office, want to be there to see him off. Take care, Prime Minister, they say, as if seeing him for the last time. The camera is silent, but we can almost hear their words: Don't let them bamboozle you, tell 'em no one wants it! And when the negotiator happily returns, having failed in his mission, they all drop everything once more and turn up to welcome him home, and I'm sure console him. But why do these people not trust *us* with anything, why don't they turn to us with a request for help couched in sincere human terms?

I often think, what will they be like in fifty or a hundred years? What measures and what gadgets will separate governments from the people? But maybe by then here, as in other countries, the governing will all be done by Japanese computers, relentlessly shaping our future and deciding the extent of our welfare. President, party secretaries, ministers will merely act out the external ritual of a European-type human government.

Yet not all that long ago the President strolled down the street outside these very Savarin windows, smiling at the bystanders while they smiled right back at him. I saw the event on TV and could hardly believe my eyes: the President seemed remarkably unguarded and uncovered, like someone who is popular. A few moments earlier he had opened the new line of the Metro, and that same day the engineers and workers had handed over to pedestrian use the crossroads of 28 October Street, Mustek and Příkopy. And it was here that the President strolled under the lindens, looking up at the windows, from which only friendly faces beamed down at him. He even stopped and, doing a better job than an American film star, chatted to the people. I was conscious of a rare sensation, welling up from inside me, a feeling not far removed from that which says that socialism might be possible in this country after all. And that if the government were only to show, more frequently and more genuinely, that it wants to do only such things as will benefit us, perhaps the nation would give up thieving and become honest again, replace greed with modesty and self-respect, apathy with self-sacrifice, idleness with diligence and learning; all that which might still remain from the days of the open and humanitarian rule of T.G. Masaryk.

What our TV showed was a 20-minute play about a republican, democratic government. It was excellently directed, so that I too was fooled at first, like the President who I suppose didn't know that only ticket-holders were allowed to enter the area. Even so, it does at least show that they still know what things *should* be like here. A vestige of a cultural consciousness, similar to a heathen doffing his hat in church. And of good manners, like when a tribunal at a political trial retires to consider the verdict.

And now I am walking, as he did, down Příkopy, looking up at the trees and all but smiling at the tits and blackbirds. Is this where we shall be sitting on benches in the spring? A row of street-lamps down the middle spread their fragile branches...I remember a photo of Příkopy taken at the end of the last century—a wide, well-lit thoroughfare, full of strolling people. After that, Příkopy went to the dogs, until there was no air and no space left, nothing but cars and trams. Now it was as if the architect had crossed out and rejected a botched blueprint and drafted a new picture of the street as it should have looked.

Looking at the other end of the pedestrian precinct, the diverse architecture and picturesque cluster of houses around Jungmann's statue, I'm suddenly put in mind of my friends who ought to see this: Jiří Gruša and Pavel Kohout, Jan Vladislav and Milan Schulz, and others from the old *Literárky*. And Jiří Kolář! Would he approve, I wonder? I only mention those with whom I at one time or another, so far as my poor memory serves me, walked along here: such as Karol Sidon and Luděk Pachman, Olda Unger, and of course Helena. But isn't it shameful and an indication of failing nerve to make such a fuss about such an obvious and belated improvement?

Suddenly I felt angry. I walked back in the other direction, from Jungmann Square to Příkopy as far as the light, clean and silent Republic Square. What has been built here, both on the surface and below ground, only goes to show, yet again, how unsuitable for our country are conditions in which character and labour are not respected but ruined, in which the human spirit is not valued but spied on and regimented. Where the government can afford to allow people in only with tickets.

I am on my way to the railway station, to welcome friends from Moravia and Slovakia. Provided they make it to town, I'll accompany them to Prague 6, where we shall be received by Zdeněk Urbánek. With some other friends we'll spend a pleasant time, discussing things that interest us. And we shan't inform the uncaring Party either!

December 1985

Coffee-house Culture

How will it all end here, in Prague and its environs? Who are the people who will live here, and will they—despite the authorities—know anything about us? Once upon a time forgetting was a private business, today it is an interest of state. And who is that state? Not we, that's for sure. A hundred or so arch-functionaries take it upon themselves to decide what is permissible in the arts, what is to happen and what is to be forgotten. And so we have no choice but to store up memory against them. Since I know and say this, shouldn't I cultivate the young rather than people like Zdeněk Urbánek? Never mind, I'll go make one more trip with him to the Union Café, since he insists.

The Union Café—ancient haunt of writers and poets like Jirásek and Vrchlický, and also Zeyer, Heyduk and Sládek. Later, Jaroslav Hašek used to sit there with Bass, and Čapek with Neumann. Hrubín recalled meeting Wolker, and of course Biebl, Nezval and Seifert, who outlived all of them in order to write about it. Urbánek, too, said: "It was one of the first coffee-houses I ever entered." Just try and translate that sentence into another language. If you don't feel how grotesquely profound it is, compose another, as for instance: "You will never again enter any of the first coffee-houses!"

It is a frosty morning, yet the sun feels hot behind the big windows of the coffee-house, as if it was spring. And here they come, the artists. As I take my seat, Zdeněk clears the table by gathering up a whole pile of magazines. "It was never this untidy at the Union Café, of course," he said. "What will you have?" I think about this, looking at the Lhoták picture on the wall opposite, showing a dirt-track motorcycle race. "I think a nice cup of tea would be nice," I reply.

While he gets things ready, I go through the magazines—they all seem to begin with "the": *The Economist, The Guardian, The Spectator, The New York Review of Books, The New York Times Book Review*, one *La Quinzaine littéraire* and one *Index on Censorship*, no "the" this time. All of them very recent, mostly from last December. I don't like homes where they try and keep up a pretence of worldliness by displaying old *Sterns* and *Spiegels*. Zdeněk puts a warmed-up cup in front of me. "I bet they never had this many newspapers at the Union Café," I say. "And tell me, doesn't the *Statesman* have the *Nation* any more?"

"The Union Café always had the latest *News Chronicle*," says Zdeněk. "The very next day, would you believe." He pours out the tea.

"I still don't have a favourite coffee-house," I say morosely. "And I don't like the way people use them. Do you really think that without coffee-houses there would have been no culture?" He thinks about this, then says: "No, of course culture wasn't *created* there, but it was an environ-

ment that encouraged it. Why, look at us, aren't we trying
to do the same?'' I got up and circled his table. ''What
is it you're writing?'' ''There you are,'' he said, smiling,
''you need to know this—sorry, maybe you don't need to
but you want to. In the old Café the younger ones used
to go and watch the older writers…'' Yes, I know, but
where will *we* be seen, I thought. And who will remember
us, when not even the younger men of the STB know about
our famous deeds? ''But you're not listening…''—''What
makes you say that?''—''You've got such a… distractedly
concentrated expression. But to come back to the *Statesman*,
when I visited their office once upon a time, I discovered
that the chief editor was a homo…''—''Don't even tell me.
But it wasn't just the Union Café, between it and the Slavia
coffee-house there was Metro and the National, which was
called Černý's in the old days…''—''It's nothing but a
waste of time, sitting around idling in cafés,'' I said
morosely; then, annoyed with myself, I added: ''Shouldn't
you be seeing younger people rather than me?''—''Why
on earth…'' he seemed puzzled, and I realised that he was
still thinking about the *Statesman*, and so I explained: ''We
shan't create any memory if we just keep talking to one
another.'' He got up from the table, smiled, and like me
began to walk about, we circled one another and I tried
to slap his bottom clad in dignified black trousers. ''I assure
you that isn't how they do it,'' he said tolerantly.—At last
I asked him: ''Will you be going to the funeral?''

He sank onto the settee and said: ''I don't know… do
you think we should go along with this farce of theirs?''—
''It does put me off, I must say,'' I told him. What it is,

I fear that genuine, profound feelings will be devalued. "The main thing," said Zdeněk, "is, I don't feel like engaging in a tug-of-war over him with *them*." I wondered whether one of us would ever describe our last visit to the late Jaroslav Seifert. Well, it won't be me, let *him* do it, after all, he's writing his memoirs. Fortunately, he's still slugging away somewhere in the fifties—at this rate he will live to a ripe old age.

"Not to mention the Danube wine cellar," Zdeněk was saying, "where the aforementioned was wont sit with Halas. One day I came there with my girl friend, who later became my wife, and I brought with me a book I'd just bought, Holan's *Triumph of Death*. Halas asked me what I was reading, so I handed the book to him and he wrote on the back: When my Zdeněk in holy ecstasy embraced the one I wished to embrace." I remembered my task. "How many rooms were there at the Union Café?"—"Six, I think, some no bigger than this room." Morosely I said: "Well, if you ask me, all it was was a glorified pub-crawl, later elevated to high cultural status." Yes, why was there no pub boasting about Březina or Bedřich Fučík? Did Jakub Deml at least frequent the Cloisters wine cellar? Once only, as far as I know, did Zdeněk lure him to the Europe Café. "There, you're not listening again—I'm talking about Medek."— "Yes, I know, Medek the poet."—"Poet and general, it's the general I'm talking about. A wonderful chap, said Halas, when he's sober, but that's only one or two days in a year. I was there, in September 1938 at the time of the mobilisation: the courier delivered his orders, the general read them, drew his sabre and began to wave it around quite dangerously in that wine cellar.''

Would this be something for our young people, I wonder. On the whole a pretty confusing tale: a poet-general. A general with poets in a wine cellar. And, moreover, a general ready to defend his homeland with his sabre as a poet.—I guess Ivan Skála would be willing to put on a general's uniform, in times of emergency, and cut us to pieces with his sabre.

It seems to me that, now that Seifert is gone, Václav Černý is the last survivor of the democratic coffee-house and of coffee-house poetry. Today is the twenty-first. In the morning two gentlemen came to urge me not to attend the funeral. The head waiter walks through the almost empty rooms of the Union Café. When the last patron gets up to go home, he will lock up.

January 1986

The Trail of the Lawman

If President Reagan was right to attack Libya, only time will tell: if there is a diminution in world terror. Naturally I, too, was shocked and at a loss how to react when I heard, and I badly needed to put some questions to the President, but where do I find him? Most of those I've spoken to condemn his action. Jiří Hájek, for instance, says it was a bullyboy gesture which the democratic world must reject and which will thus serve only to benefit the Soviet Union. That seems to me true enough, and yet isn't it just on the slow response of the democracies that dictators and their terrorists rely? In which case is it not sensible and laudable to pay them back in their own coin for a change? Let us suppose that the President has proof (and this is what I would have liked to have asked him about) that the evil stems from Libya. But even then, thinks František Vodsloň, the Americans should have dispatched secret commando units to track the terrorists down and capture them. An excellent idea, but what if this is something they have already been doing to no effect? A sort of gang war, in which it is again innocent people who perish, not knowing on whose behalf and by whose hand. That is why I ask myself whether such a daring open counter-attack, admittedly risky from a political point of view but victoriously cleansing if successful, is not morally preferable, providing a general catharsis. Someone to their shame has done for us what we often, in our righteous anger, would like to do ourselves.

For the time being, though, I appear to be in a minority of one. I'm puzzled by Zdeněk Urbánek's opinion. He doesn't like President Reagan but likes terrorists even less; on the other hand he once said, referring to the peasants living by the Elbe, that humanitarians should be hanged; is it just shooting he objects to? And I have no idea what Šimečka thinks about Reagan's action, since when I last saw him in Bratislava it had not happened yet.

I have always liked the idea of obtaining justice cowboy-fashion. Or in the manner of Robin Hood. When everyone in the saloon can see who is in the right, then the man who allows himself to be bullied is finished. Like most people in this country I have had more than enough opportunity to study the question of ''civil courage'' and I believe that we all would be able, without a teacher's assistance, to award ourselves the appropriate, secret marks. The more appropriate, the more secret. My secret mark would not be the highest. Do I have to explain why?

Well, because in the end, when all is done and despite everything I say, I accept the conditions we have to live in: and I live in them. True, I have to face overwhelming odds, avoid traps, I try and distract the opponent's attention elsewhere, sometimes I speak up cautiously, at others I keep silent just to exist. And so I go on existing, even though I ought long ago to have perished while executing justice. We talk about our rights and invoke the law of the land in the belief that it has a validity of its own and is duty-bound to come to our aid. But where is the law to derive its strength: from the paper on which it is written? Who is to force the bureaucrats administering the law to act in its spirit? No one, and nothing, but brute force. Just take a look at the courts—and to get *there* we would have to use our fists!—and listen to their judgements. What kind of justice is this? ''Luke halted on top of the hill and looked around. Then slowly he rode down towards the land that had long been waiting for a lawman...''

The day after I arrived in Bratislava I left it again, against my will. Milan Šimečka was waiting for me on the platform, though we had already made our forced farewells earlier; he had brought me my razor and shaving brush, which I had left behind. As he walked towards me, two young men started shoving him away, at the same time telling me not to stop. They behaved as if they were a couple of grown-ups, and Milan and I children, or as if we were a pair of criminals and they honest citizens, as if they were white South Africans and Milan and I no-account stinking blacks, or as if they were two SS-men on the ramp of a concentration camp and we a couple of wretched Pressburg Jews: you over there, and you there!

The train thundered in just as one of the emissaries was pushing Milan away from me towards the rails, Milan resisting and tottering on the edge of the platform. To put an end to this dangerous game I took the razor and brush from him and said goodbye, walking on along the train as it applied its brakes. The two young hooligans followed me.

(For the benefit of the foreign reader let me say that Milan Šimečka and I had not committed any crime, and therefore had no reason to consider those two bastards to be men of the law. I cannot even swear that they actually *were* security men. And I thus have to ask myself shamefacedly why did I not hit out at them?)

I found an empty compartment and sat down. One of the young thugs asked to see the razor and brush. I was curious to discover what was behind this, and so I handed them over. On the surface, this young Bratislava fellow looked quite normal, and I'm sure that when they meet him in the street people treat him like any other European. Maybe he even has a wife. The poor woman probably doesn't know that her man spends entire days hatching intrigues and sniffing out things. Today, for example, he mingled among adults at the railway station and was now bothering an elderly traveller: "Can I see that brush and razor?"

I ask myself who could have been the parents of such people? They know not honour and have no respect for courage, relying in their work on cowards, weaklings, stool-pigeons, corrupt and degenerate people. What kind of a brain do they have that they don't need to look at things from two sides, are blind both to history and to the future, allow themselves to remain uneducated and uninformed? Were they born like that, or did they let themselves be destroyed later? To whom do they, as human beings, feel accountable—not, God forbid, to their superiors? For if that were the case, only one word would stand between us and the great terror: orders.

He inspects my shaving brush, then he knocks it several times against the wall of the compartment: rap, rap rap. Arrogant ignorance pours out of his head over his jacket and trousers, onto the floor, the stench stays with us all the way to Prague. Let him who once again is bringing home a bad secret mark suffer the smell.

April 1986

My Birthday Present

I opened the door—and it was as if I had bumped into a pillar just inside the room. It quite took my breath away: on the wall facing me there hung a huge portrait of myself, at least a metre in size. My friends who sat in the room were watching me, maliciously I thought, and my first instinct was to cover my face, but what was the use, it stared at us from the wall, large as life. Casting a quick eye around the room, I realised that they weren't actually laughing at me, rather waiting expectantly to see how I would react. I plucked up the courage to take a closer look: the portrait was of a middle-aged fellow, seen in profile, with greying hair, an interestingly furrowed face, dashingly dishevelled moustache, his eye half-hidden in the shadows. Yes, it was I all right, but somehow more sympathetic-looking, though quite faithfully portrayed.

"Isn't that good," I said.

"It's splendid," said Eda Kriseová.

"Well, it's you, all right," said Milan Jungmann.

My initial shock over, I began to be pleased: that my friends had called upon the talent and skill of Josef Zeman, who had painted this huge picture in his spare time—he

cleaned out horses' stables during working hours—and no doubt with too little time to do it in. I went over to the portrait and touched the canvas. The tempera was still damp, and at the edges you could discern the grid Josef had used to help him transfer my likeness from the tiny slide to this somewhat more monumental format. The present surprised me, and I like it, so I'll wait until the Šimečkas and the Kusýs have had a chance to see it before I put it away. It'll then rest behind the wardrobe and I'll bring it out to show to anyone who may be interested.

It is quite a blow to see your own face lording it on high. Pity poor Stalin, once upon a time, and Gottwald and Novotný, eternally dragged through the streets. Or were they inured to this? Maybe they thought so little of themselves that it did them good. Or again, they had said to themselves at the outset: I serve! I wonder how it feels to have your face canceled every day on thousands of postal stamps?

Looking at your own face is, for normal people, an intimate experience. I do it for about three minutes each day, when I shave. I no longer give any thought to what I see in the mirror, unless it is to ask myself if I should at last get rid of that moustache. I started growing it as a bit of a joke, and only as a temporary measure: until the day the Russians go home. And while they have apparently resigned themselves to their unending sojourn, I have never come to terms with my disguise. No, a man should not change either his face or his religion. Why then do I tolerate that handsome appendage? Because women, whatever their relationship with me, all think that it suits me. Which is silly and immoral, the least of my immoralities. But one of these days I'll mend my ways and shave it off, thus incidentally also proclaiming my independence of female opinion. Two years ago I attended an old boys' dinner in Zlín: I found my former classmates changed in all manner of ways but not a single one had resorted to a moustache. That really made me think.

It has occurred to me that perhaps I'm cultivating my father's moustache. He had grown one from the time of his adolescence and never changed his appearance thereafter. When I shave I also think that now I have lived three years longer than he did. I ask myself how and why this should be so. I keep returning to his face and his voice, I can feel myself making his gestures. In my speech I can hear his tones. My worries seem to me like his, I measure my stamina and capabilities against his. I envy him (in the nicest way) that he managed to see more of the world than I, but I don't envy him his hard life, responsibility and meagre reward. He is now my younger brother, and I cannot understand how I could have been so strict with him when I was thirty. I believe I have advanced further in knowledge than he, and I have a better life. I wonder if he could see me now, what he would say to me and what he expects of me, will I have time to live up to his expectations. Will I choose the right moment? Am I capable of the ultimate sacrifice?

That is, I'm still working on my portrait, just for myself. I grow older, but like my father I ignore it. Not that I don't realise it, but there are adventures still in store. True, but now I have no more taste for danger and uncertainty. I cling to my certainties, though getting ready to lose them. Since I never really chose a profession, I go on writing, but I'm not really a writer, or I'd write more and with greater gusto. (Even this I'm writing in September instead of July because I was afraid of the invasion anniversary theme and kept putting it off.)

And so I tidied away Josef's present, asking my friends to forgive me. The incident reminded me of my dilemmas back in 1967 and the following year: all I wanted was to say something, but it turned out to be a much more public affair with long repercussions. Fame rhymes with shame, and you cannot remove the hook from your own mouth without losing a bit of flesh. Why, then, don't I shut up now? Once and for all? Simply because I've never known how to do that, nor did I wish to. Hearing this, one of my friends sitting under that wretched portrait said: "Why then do you refuse to become one of the Charter spokesmen?"

I had no choice but to grin and bear it. I know well enough why, but I would not say it, and I won't write it here either. I am tempted to pull that picture from behind the wardrobe and kick it for punishment. I ask the picture—we only communicate via the wardrobe—whether the total anonymity of work is not the one and only virtue. For that, replies the picture, you have to have the necessary character. Kosík is the wise one, writing and going on writing while people believe he has given up, his faith in the meaning behind all that labour quietly resting in the *oeuvre* itself, whose worth will only become clear in time, when Kosík may or may not be around to see it. Only those who act behind the scenes, murmurs the wardrobe, are guaranteed modesty. How about working in the public view, I argue, but without reward or remuneration. If you ask for nothing you're free to do what you like. And the picture answers: Freedom, that's the excuse of all selfish people. Add hard work and at least you do have an excuse. Better a good excuse than a dog's turd, Josef would say if he were here.

He has found the best solution: serving horses so that he doesn't have to serve people and the state. Alone, unknown, free and modest. Modest? the wardrobe mocks me. If he wants to stay modest, let him stick to his manure and not paint portraits!

July 1986

A Day in August

"We've got nothing to welcome them with," said my cousin Ludvík that August morning. "We've drunk all the *slivovitz*, and we have no grenades."

That day was as long as a black night, sleepless and helpless. It seemed incredible that the sun should, as usual, cross the heavens, the train pass by, and the bakers bake the bread. What, we wondered, was happening back in Prague? The radio kept broadcasting in a shaky voice, while from behind the bushes in the frontier regions its language was permeated with nonsensical phrases of a kind the Czech tongue had only recently rid itself of. Surely we're never going to speak like this again, I said to myself the next day as I listened. On the third day, gazing at Ludvík's radio on top of the sideboard, it seemed to me that our government had been saved, our defences were growing stronger. But we should have to think up a new name for socialism, it can't show itself in public with the old name any more. It felt strange to be so completely out of things—to be as unimportant as are (and always have been) all these relatives and friends of mine here in Brumov.

However, let's stay with that first day. What did I do,

unable to do anything? I left Ludvík's, where I was staying, to visit my old teacher, who was putting my wife up. They had turned off the radio, reception was lousy. The old lady displayed a strange calm, just as she had during the war.

The house all around us seemed terribly oppressive, so we went out. Across the railway-line and up into the woods: silence, the smell of grass, an August sky, and cows far away on the hilltop opposite. When I later returned to Prague, everyone told me about the roar of engines and the stink of the tanks' diesel fumes. Here, nothing but wild mushrooms. But there was no getting away from it, I could not cheat my way out of my collapsing world by pretending I belonged here. I felt sick, and I'll never forget how, despite the sensation of panic in my stomach, head and legs, I was conscious of a fatalistic sense of relief, resigned to the inevitable. Just then, my wife, walking behind me, said: "Don't be scared." There was absolutely no reason not to be scared, quite the contrary. So what she really must have meant was: "Grin and bear it." Put up with your fear.

In Prague, later, it seemed to me that those who had been present when things were happening had had an easier time of it. For example, Karol Sidon had ignored the tanks and carried on putting out *Literární listy*. And others did other things. Many and excellent. Here, on top of the hill, there was nothing but a fierce autumnal wind from the East. The kind that in a thousand years will turn the mountains into a plain—without violence. I gazed towards the green East, where, beyond the mountains there were more mountains, beyond the plains, more plains, beyond the rivers...

tundra far and wide. What could be done about it, what is our fate now going to be and, should we survive, what our mission? Thank God I'm only what I am! How ashamed I'd have to feel if earlier I had been influential beyond my powers and capabilities—now all power and influence would have been gone, only responsibility remained. As it is, I'm the same as I was before, and I can stand by all I said.

It was late afternoon when we returned to the old teacher's house, where we found Ludvík waiting for us with a man dressed in gamekeeper's uniform. Ludvík introduced us and said that the lads in the factory were of the opinion that I ought to make myself scarce and hide. This chap was going to take me to a safe place where no one would find me in a month of Sundays. I said no, and both my old teacher and my wife said no, surely that wasn't necessary yet.

Next day I was visited at Ludvík's by one of the factory workers. Would I come and give a talk in their workshop. I don't remember what I said to them, though I can well imagine what it was. In any case, I knew that words were useless. Had they ever been any use? On the other hand, they *are* useful if they concentrate the mind and organise what strength there is without overdoing it. How stupid it is when those who were so full ideas when all was well, have nothing to say for themselves when trouble strikes. But there is one thing each and every one of us can do, at any time—refuse to eat our words.

Attending a meeting at the Law Faculty in Prague, I lacked the fighting experience of the streets, and I disappointed the students when I told them we would have to accept whatever was happening. We were like people, the fruit of whose labours had been destroyed by a thunderstorm, but what if our real task was a different one, and what if it was only just beginning? Through us Europe will pour eastwards. (Let us leave aside the question of what kind of Europe it is.)

It was I think some time in 1970 that a young man of my acquaintance came to see me, saying that in these difficult times when there was no organised opposition everyone had to choose their own tactics. As far as he was concerned, he had decided to sacrifice his good name and join the Party; he will then be able to build up some kind of a position and save the work of his friends and colleagues who, it seemed, were all going to be fired, leaving the field to weaklings and incompetents interested only in promotion. He had come to tell me about it as he could not bear to keep it to himself. I replied that I thought it was possible to do what he was thinking of doing, but that it was dangerous and only the final outcome would tell. We both of us, of course, imagined that the outcome would be known sooner. So, to cut a long story short, let me tell you that his experiment is still in progress. I often think of him but we must not see each other. One day we are bound to find out the result.

I think of them all. For a long time it seemed to me that there must be people like that even in the government. To this day, surprising though it may seem, I don't condemn even the President. If I am unable, or not allowed to function, I have to grin and bear it. Let them get on with it.

But I don't have to keep silent, that I don't! Just last it out here until such a time ... I frequently wonder how it is possible that this entire collapse, this national disaster, started with several seemingly decent, from a political point of view understandable and voluntary resignations. And then the sewers down below opened. However, there can be no doubt that whatever has been done that is good, has been done by those who were able to take a hand, and who had managed to hang on to the remnants of their integrity. And whatever has been done that is rotten, is the fault of the weak, the nasty and the treacherous.

Above all, I asked myself how come we had not been liquidated or exiled to some faraway places. That, too, was somebody's doing. Undoubtedly they must have discussed it. At that time our fate depended on how well they had grasped their mission.

No one publicly celebrates that August day: neither we, nor they, nor *they*. Occasionally I celebrate (?) it, just for myself. As the day my mission became clear to me. That evening, cousin Ludvík had said: "If only they'd leave before too long. While there are still flowers."

Flowers to say farewell with—let's keep them handy, all the time.

August 1986

A Few Words of Advice for the British Government

You could hear a pin drop in the cinema as the three-hour-long Anglo-Indian film about Mahatma Gandhi nears its end, a film that could easily give audiences ideas about rising to overthrow our very own Raj, so much so that I'm surprised they allow it to be shown. I never cease to be amazed at the way they delight in showing us other people's cruelties and injustices, as if they themselves were pure as the driven snow. The audience, and in particular the young ones among them, follow the action on the screen with attentive enthusiasm and no doubt gain much food for thought—dangerous, good thoughts which will go on maturing with time. I certainly hope so.

I have long been of the opinion that for a nation like ours, which lacks the numbers and the terrain to be able to take violent action in keeping with its need, Gandhi's notion of *satiagraha* (non-violent resistance) could point the way to *svaraj* (self-administration). Now that large cinema audiences are in a position to know far more about Gandhi's thoughts and politics than we did when we were merely able to read about them, I confess that it was Gandhi I had very much in mind back in 1967, and it was with him at my elbow that a year later I wrote my "Two Thousand Words" when, unprepared, I was challenged by a number of my compatriots to answer the question WHAT TO DO NOW. No one at that time recognised where my inspiration had come from, except for one Englishman, who published my non-violently aggressive text; I still have the translation somewhere. It has remained my little secret, which it was easy for me to keep, since I'd never have dared to admit to so exotic an impulse. And doubtless most people would have derided me for it—what a daft idea, Gandhi may have been all right for India but hardly for us. Yet I am convinced that the Indian Gandhi *is* for us, at least in the European conception behind the film about his life.

It goes without saying that there has always been a considerable difference between ancient Indian philosophy and European Christianity, although the Christian precept on how to deal with evil is not that far removed from Hinduism. But now that Europeans are becoming alienated from their Christian faith, what has Gandhi to say to us? And, in any case, India itself has left him some way behind. Judging by the way filmgoers have reacted to the film about Gandhi, it has something to tell them of normal human morality, a moral authority which works in a modern, political fashion. We must not, however, lose sight of the fact that the social conditions which gave rise to Gandhi's moral authority were those of abject poverty. We have to try and imagine what kind of anti-British resistance would have been put up by well-dressed and well-fed Indians.

This alone shows that our objection to *our* "Brits" is on a higher, more spiritual plane. And maybe we shouldn't even object. They give us almost everything they have themselves, you might say. What then should our resistance be like, what form should it take? All we need, really, is the knowledge—and each one of us will have it in varying degrees and use different arguments to express it—that we human beings must not give way to organised evil. Those of us who feel this strongly are obviously further along that road than those who are content with their share of bread and circuses. And it matters little whether we are motivated mainly by a thirst for Truth, the obligation of Honour, a need for Order, or obedience to God. Who comes closer to salvation: a poor, hungry wretch with just a single idea in his head, or the man who has all he needs but is thinking of something else? Yes, I know what the Bible has to say on this subject, but try and think it out for yourself. Not forgetting the question why the poor wretches, when moved by religious fervour, tend to resort to arson and murder so that, instead of in paradise, they wake up in some kind of communism.

And because of all that, I believe—paradoxically perhaps—that Gandhi today is more topical for us here than for his native India. Unnamed and undetected, he has been present, so to speak, spontaneously: was his spirit not there in our streets in the August of 1968? And can you not discern him behind the ideas of Charter 77? An unknown but quite large number of adequately clothed and fed men and women daily realise what is right and what is wrong, and they are willing to sacrifice something for this, if someone tells them where and how. And so the only thing missing is a Gandhi to lead us, but no one wants to play that role. Why, I don't know. Lack of courage, perhaps, for such a terrible modesty. And what about communications? And, furthermore, we know that if the idea were to be given a human form, it would inevitably be that of Jan Palach.*

But let's stay in the cinema. All I wanted was to share with you the thoughts that came to me while watching the film. I am not knowledgeable enough, nor strong enough, to follow the weighty thoughts I touched on above to their conclusion. Oh, and let me not forget to say how relieved I was to find that the Mahatma, that great old ascetic, had a sense of humour. "We are not going to strike, we shall just spend the day at prayer," or words to that effect. So, I says to myself, we don't have to go to the trouble of demonstrating in protest, let's simply fox the power works by switching off all our appliances at home. We are in a position to ruin entire industries by refraining from buying their products. I also think about empty corridors in all the official buildings, as I did twenty years ago. Only my head has grown heavier since.

What really struck me in the cinema was the weakness of the British Government. Someone like Gandhi could exist only under British oppression. Look at him, beaten up, he still goes on burning identity cards with a shaking hand— why didn't they put him away for five years or so? Or why did they not raid his *ashram* and confiscate his books? And then he and his followers throw themselves on the ground in front of the cavalry—why, any one of our dissidents could

*Czech student leader who burned himself to death in January 1969 in protest at the Soviet invasion.

easily do the same. Those people lacked our certainty that we would be run over by some inhuman horse. And what about that moving—though in our eyes absurd—scene in the courtroom? The judge, obviously unfit for the job, sympathises with the accused, who is cheered by the spectators; how come the room was full of ordinary people instead of British secret policemen? And in the end General Smuts revokes his law—an elementary mistake! Never revoke anything, even if they were to promote you for it. Or take the scene where Gandhi arrives somewhere by train, the multitude welcomes him, and then one of the two soldiers present fights his way towards him to say "You're under arrest!" "For what?" asks Gandhi, whereupon the Englishman, confused by the logic behind that question, backs away. I was tempted to jump to my feet and shout "For nothing, we just felt like it! We'll show you!" And when, at long last, they put him in prison...they allow journalists to visit him and write about it. Why, in heaven's name, doesn't that government do something about its prisons and its press! And finally, instead of having him run over or drowned in the Vistula River, MacDonald, would you believe, actually invites him to London. It is only at the end, when he is killed by his own people, that we feel at home again. The government was an alien one, the murderer is one of us.

So we have got our murderer. Will we succeed in finding a Gandhi for him? Well, I think even that is possible. I certainly hope so.

October 1986

Words...

Once again I've reached an impasse with my writing: what good is it doing anyone? What good is it doing me, for that matter? It doesn't help to solve anything, I can't see that it affects anything at all. That is why I am once again tempted to give it up and later, after a useful pause, perhaps take up something else. Something new. I once tried, with the help of a few friends, to make up my mind what that something should be, but as soon as I broached the subject, the only response was an embarrassed silence. Nevertheless, I haven't given up the idea, and now I think I may be on the verge of something!

Maybe I'll start my own school, I think I'd enjoy that. A perit...peripatetic school in which nothing needs to be written or read, perhaps not even known. A school in which the pupils gain enlightenment from their master's every idea or invention, sensible or nonsensical, even his every mood, experience, adventure or misadventure. Where everything he touches or comes across can become a teaching aid. In such a school in the open air everything can be quickly put in its right perspective and the world pointed in the right direction towards a better future. But this writing of mine...it's been dragging on uselessly for such a long time.

I know: it counts as a success if the author at least entertains his readers, gives them a little encouragement or some new ideas. But I'm not interested in entertaining people, and in any case how many can I hope to reach in this way? It's hardly worth doing for thirty or two hundred heads. True, it *would* be worthwhile to discover new horizons, provide interesting impulses, even for a handful of readers...but how can I do that in our conditions? Can I provide even one a year? And anyway, who is asking me to do this, what gives me the right? It seems to me that this writing of mine probably only serves as an excuse for me not to do something more useful.

There are many of us who go on writing like this, and some of them I read and admire: what gives them the confidence that it is all still worth doing—in a wider sense than just for one's own personal satisfaction? What is Milan Šimečka after? He wants to define conditions and describe phenomena... Why? All we are doing is sweeping general knowledge and experience up into a snowdrift which we hope will one day turn into an avalanche and engulf the main culprits. Now, that would be fine, but is that in fact what will happen? Not by itself, it won't. First you need an earth tremor. And who is going to shake the ground? Some event or explosion which we can only wait for. And so we wait for some event—these days mere words will not shake the earth.

An old question, this: what price the word? When I was more naive, stronger, healthier and purer I truly thought that all one had to do was to find the right word, the word that would contain the truth, act as a challenge, forge a weapon. I was to discover—and I'm by no means alone in this—that the word remains but a word unless you have the weapon to back it up. And so, what is the use of still more words without weapons? And what use would even weapons be against overwhelming odds. Suicide by a foreign hand?

And yet even now, depending on my state of mind, I sometimes think about The Word. I think about it when I learn of suppressed reports about the devastation of our environment, about the (badly planned) growth of industry, about the enforced merger of villages and agricultural cooperatives, about the immoral privileges of our leading socialists, the greedy ways of the gang of directors, the venality of our TV, film and literary puppets, our artificial scientists and incapable businessmen... I find The Word, and relinquish it. It is too dangerous to utter. More than that, it would be irresponsible to do so. And if you can't be responsible, all that is left is delusions of grandeur, and immodesty. Yet, all this—danger, responsibility, immodesty—one can shoulder, provided there is at least some chance of success. But is there?

I relinquish The Word also because it is in no way original and my own. On the contrary, everyone else knows and possesses it. So that it isn't a question of The Word but rather of the right moment to launch it, that flash which will illuminate the entire landscape; something that will not ever happen because it has never happened. The landscape proves to be too effective an insulator when the population at large remains endlessly apathetic and does not want to see any change in the *status quo*. I relinquish The Word when I see that the majority of us are content—or at the very least resigned. Whom am I to address? How to address those who daily choose the immediate personal advantage in preference to the future of mankind? Tropical forests are on fire, the desert encroaches. All humanity, if you like, is harmful. What is one to say to this? Try walking more?

And so this year—but also the year before last—despite what I may have said in coffee-houses, it is the so-called nation and not the government which has for fifteen years now seemed to me like a heavy, immovable boulder. The people! The football crowd. Our consumer, that large, futile mass that swears at "the conditions" but does nothing. It is at them that The Word should be aimed, but what right have we to do that? In any case, we cannot possibly reach them with the means we have at our disposal today, while they, in their ignorance or apathy, make no effort to reach us. They, not the government, are the chief obstacle on the road (whose?) to... What? Let us say, for the time being: to a condition of equilibrium... no, that should read: to a condition of equilibrium of Earth as a whole, and to great diversity in its individual components.

One summer day, on a tram, I heard a little boy of about ten ask his mother: "Where is infinity? I mean, in our country?" His mother leaned forward to tell him, but I failed to hear what she said. From time to time I think of that boy and would like to know what has happened to him. Yes, he got it right, that was the proper question to ask: where do you find infinity, I mean, in our country?

I know of one, my lad. Come afterwards.

February 1986

POSTSCRIPT

Glasnost

Glasnost

Corrupt minister put on trial, sentenced and executed. Committee of something or other jeered at. Head of secret police punished for trying to suppress a newsman's criticism. Factory workers discussing management problems in their factory. Coca-Cola becoming part of socialist reconstruction. Banned films taken off the shelf. Theatres now belong to those who act in them. Monstrous project to reverse the course of rivers cancelled. Honour and conscience reinstated.

I observe all this in sceptical suspense, as a socialist, and with some derision, as a Czech. So they again think they're better than us. And again on the basis that might is right. True, that country has needed for a long time for someone to come and shake it up, and yet it's all rather sad: by the time an idea has been grasped by the Russian bureaucrat, it is hardly new where the rest of the world is concerned. We saw this in cybernetics forty years ago, later it was jazz, and now—well, now we are being presented with the Moscow version of the 1968 Prague Spring. Our people are understandably puzzled, asking one another what's in it for us.

For my own person I expect nothing, nor do I intend to wait for it.

At the same time I watch our government reluctantly giving us information and trying to calm down expectations: don't worry, nothing as momentous as that is going to happen here. After all, every country has the right to go its own way, courageously declared Bilak. There you are then—all these years we have longed for a government that would not act as someone's arse-lickers, and now we have got it! Is this not indeed a historic moment? Our government is resolved to stand its ground, sit on it, even lie on it if necessary. And it has my support, because I am a patriot. And as such I know full well that, even if Bilak says so, it is true that we don't have to (we never did in the past and won't have to in a thousand years) slavishly follow the Soviet model. Whatever happens in that land of the present wonders, we shall still have the right, as we always had, to do our own thing. For that, we don't need any Gorbachev; just as we don't need Bilak to tell us that we shouldn't have to slavishly follow *his* model, either. Let's not beat about the bush—we can do without the two of them. So that, should Moscow now order us to be allowed freedom, I'll resist.

I am reminded of recent developments in the case of Jan Hus: the Catholic Church, having matured to embrace his teaching, intends to canonise him. As a Catholic, I ought to view this as a victory for truth, integrity, and the Holy Spirit. But I can't help thinking: ''I wonder what the dead on both sides of the conflict will make of this: 'The powers-that-be will always come to terms in the end. We should've bided our time and lived!' ''

Ethical considerations apart, does not this intention on the part of the Church also betray a noetic failing? Let's look at the whole thing realistically: the two thousand-year-old Church gropes with its now living, becalmed limbs way back into the fifteenth century and preaches something at its then living, agitated limbs. The bloody, holy struggle is suddenly devalued by a messenger from Rome telling us that the cause of the conflict is no longer a burning issue and that the Church is no longer interested. I think that Hus himself, if he does not want to disappoint us, must today say to them: "Leave me be, I'm not interested in your concerns, I have other things on my mind." What other things, that is what the Church should be worrying about: What is its nice, new saint cooking up against it now?

What a marvellous theological, philosophical and moral problem this is. What I don't like about it is that they are trying to solve it by means of a politico-bureaucratic decision. Having failed to acknowledge their victim's bit of truth at the time, they would now rob him of it. All of a sudden they wish to serve the truth, which has in the meantime moved on and has other business to attend to.

So, what to do about Hus? If you're asking me, nothing. Leave things as they are, where they ended up in so instructive a conflict. It seems to me that the truth about the Church and man which came out of that conflict is probably more important than the truth which gave rise to the conflict in the first place.

Hus's sacred words can now do nothing but harmfully encourage all the heretics and dissidents who would cheerfully go to the stake, or burn others, for their truth rather than abide by it and live it modestly, without going down in history. As a Hussite, it seems to me that it would have been simply boring to snuff it without a flame, merely through some disease or old age, without anything to show for it, no obvious success, no persecution and torment.

I gaze in astonishment at that inaccessible land which is now with great hullaballoo, opening its state mines to excavate the truth. With hullaballoo, making a song and dance about it, but also with considerable charm which—I hope, as a European—can fool only the Americans. And as our Holy See rummages in our trunk of 1968 vintage, a disgust wiser than I clamours to be heard inside me, whispering: ''It's OK. It was *their* trunk, wasn't it.'' And I, old fool that I am, shake my head in disbelief, wondering how come I didn't realise this all those years ago when I was still a young fool.

To manufacture quality goods: what a revolutionary and daring idea. More than one candidate to stand for election: now there's a discovery for you. And grow vegetables on your very own private patch. Independent thought, too—for how long, this time? Conscience to be your highest guide: even if it goes against the grain? But no, we wish you every success, carry on and more power to your elbow. There are still more amazing discoveries waiting to be made: for instance, the separation of legislative, executive and judicial power. But whatever you may discover, just leave us alone, especially if you don't feel like it.

Nevertheless, I am of the opinion that, Bilak and me notwithstanding, we'll not escape being hit by some of the rocks from that truth-quarry of theirs. That is inevitable when the big and the small make music together. Something is bound to come out of it. I have already read the memorandum penned by Čestmír Císař—sensible and well-reasoned... well, let us say, political. If things are to move here at all, perhaps it will this time be from Císař here to Mlynář out there... It reminds me of the old joke about the poor Jew who complains to his rabbi about the cramped conditions in his little cottage. And so the rabbi advises him, first to bring his goat into his living room, then his pig, and finally his cow. The Jew does as the rabbi says, but things go from bad to worse. He goes back to the rabbi, complaining that now life is completely unbearable. And the rabbi says, get rid of the animals and put them back in the sty. The Jew does so and breathes a great sigh of relief at the space he now has in his cottage.

What I'm leading up to with all this is just to say that I, as a socialist, *will* derive a certain satisfaction from any new reform movement that might yet come into being here, unlikely as it may sound. Yes, I would feel a certain relief, just like that poor Jew.

February 1987